The Old Man
and
His Soul

Farida Sharan

Wisdome Press

Wisdome Press is a Division of:
School of Natural Medicine International
4645 North Broadway Street, Boulder, Colorado 80304 USA
Telephone: 720 746-9961   Fax: 303 755-3167

Web: www.faridasharan.com   www.purehealth.com
Blog: www.independentlyhealthy.typepad.com

Published in trade paper in 2010 by Wisdome Press
1 2 3 4 5 6 7 8 9 10

India Rights: Akshaya Prakashan, 2/18 Ansari Road, New Delhi 110 002
Telephone: 011-232 78034 Email: harish@akshayaprakashan.com

 Library of Congress Control Number: 2010925064

Sharan, Farida
        The Old Man and His Soul/Farida Sharan
        p.cm
        Includes glossary
        ISBN 9781452852140
        1. Spirituality 2. Religion 3. Mysticism 4. India 5. Death & Dying
        6. Transformation 7. Sadhu 8. Hindu 9. Self Actualization
        (Psychology). I.Title

Printed and bound in Boulder, Colorado in the United State of America

DEDICATION

I dedicate this book
to the divine source
that gifted me
with the dream
of the old man.

I share this story
to inspire others
to envision
their departure from this world
as an adventure,
and participate with courage
and devotion
toward union
with their soul.

All paths lead Home.

TABLE OF CONTENTS

THANK YOU

Beloved Lord of my Soul for the dream;

Dear spiritual companions for encouraging me;

Doug Childers for inspiring me;

Dearest daughter Chalice for superb editing;

Dearest daughter Casel for passionate support;

Laurel Kallenbach for proofreading;

Carolyn Oakley for designing the book;

Dilarom Asimova, for introducing me to Kashi Pandita;

Kashi, for introducing me to your publisher;

Shri Harish Chandra, for publishing this book in India;

Thank you for the love that sustains

the grace that gifts

dancing

in the hands of

God.

REFUGE IN THE HOLY CITY

The old man knew he needed to find shelter. After shivering through the night, he sought warmth in a roadside café. Holding a cup of steaming *chai* to warm his hands, and trembling with the cold that seeped into his bones, he knew he could no longer live outside. For a moment fear flew through him. Would he have to return to his ancestral home? No, the time left to him was not long, and he knew he must continue his search for a spiritual teacher and a true path to guide him on the journey of his soul.

Although he had faced hardships as he wandered through the country pathways and small villages of northern India, the old man had accepted discomforts with patience, as they were part of the adventure and the freedom, but as autumn shivered toward winter, cold had become his enemy. Instead of sleeping under a tree or by a stream, as he had through the spring and summer, he stayed closer to the villages, exchanging small tasks for a night in a shed or permission to curl up beside a fire.

The old man turned his mind from fear as the anticipation of another day of pilgrimage made his heart sing. Always the thought that perhaps today was the day went though his mind as he put on his sandals and made ready for the road.

Letting thoughts go, he strode along a dirt path onto a busy road thundering with *tuk tuks*, motorcycles, beeping taxis, and trucks painted with pink lotuses and slogans like 'God is Love'. Shabby buses, packed full of passengers and laden with suitcases, their drivers facing pictures of gurus as hopeful protection against the fear of accidents and the rage of passengers, loomed dangerously in the heavy traffic. On both sides of the road, schoolchildren, servants, students, office workers, and housewives stepped around mounds of construction and refuse to shop in the bustling markets or wait in long lines at bus stops. Vehicles did their best to avoid mangy dogs, elaborately decorated camels, occasional weary elephants, wandering distracted cows, and the children who raced amongst the chaos, holding babies decorated with kohl black eyes as they begged drivers and passengers for alms. Teams of young boys advanced aggressively to wash car windows or sell flower garlands to passengers whenever confusion or congestion halted progress.

Even though the noise, dust, and pollution overwhelmed the old man, he could not get enough of the sights, scents and sounds of his mother country. Even amongst the chaos, his eyes delighted in the glimpses of school children shining with promise as they skipped to school, freshly scrubbed, their ebony hair gleaming with oil and he admired the quiet dignity of young mothers swaying in cotton saris – their babies on their hips. Village girls chattered as they carried their produce to market, showing off bright floral skirts and blouses in mango, magenta, pink and persimmon, their shawls glittering with sparkly trims. In contrast, serious businessmen wearing suits or black pants and white shirts, and carrying briefcases, walked with detached purpose through the noise, color and dust of the crowds.

The old man felt the hungry eyes of shopkeepers and merchants scanning the crowds for customers, and the more desperate need of farmers and their wives as they laid their produce and crafts on the ground. Here and there amongst the crowds, a maimed beggar or a holy man leaned against a wall, waiting for the will of God to provide. "Isn't that what we are all doing?" he thought, "Waiting for God, whether we know it or not? What do we know of the next day, or the next hour? We are helpless before what is to come."

He was startled from his thoughts by a current of laughter that ran through the crowd when a tiny piglet broke free and ran helter-skelter through the traffic. Its owners chased the piglet as vehicles screeched to a halt. Crowds gathered to watch, laughing and pointing until the tiny piglet was caught, and then the stream of movement flowed again. Although it seemed that everyone was focused on their own goals, the old man acknowledged the awareness that enabled everyone who was a part of the orchestrated chaos to adjust as they made their way to their destinations. "Ah, this is India," he sighed, as he made his way out of the town.

As the old man glimpsed the lives of the people, he was also aware of the poignant future of infants and the impending passing of the elders, the illusions of the rich and the struggles of the poor, the fragile gift of the healthy and the pain of the sick, the temporary happiness of lovers and the sorrow of those who had suffered loss. He accepted all with a love that respected the mystical unknown. Though chaos seemed to reign, he felt instinctively that something greater was in charge. He was a seeker of God playing his part in the symphony of life. His role as a spiritual seeker was an ancient and honored one and his increasing love for the peoples of his country seemed to be part of that journey.

Leaving the bustling early morning life of the town with relief, the old man hiked vigorously through the spare, wintering lands punctuated by concrete dwellings, village temples, and farm buildings. At a crossroads, he came across men, women, and children with bedrolls balanced on their heads and bundles slung across their shoulders. He walked behind them for a time, and then as others joined the group, he merged into a stream of pilgrims and was carried along with their joy.

A little boy asked his father if he would receive blessed food. A strong young man looked proud when his father said, "We will give service to the Master." Mothers seemed uplifted with anticipation as they carried their babies. Young children, eyes closed and mouths open, slept on their fathers' backs or held hands with brothers and sisters and skipped along. The elderly moved more slowly, supported by canes or the arms of stronger, younger family members, yet their faces glowed with happiness. One old lady repeated, "Master," her face shining with love. Shy teenage girls stayed close to their parents, peeking at young men from behind their scarves or chattering among themselves.

The crowd swelled as though a magnet were gathering and pulling them toward a place of power. The old man's heart beat fast with anticipation, but he did not ask any questions, as that was his nature. It was enough for him to know he was heading toward a holy place.

When the spires of a temple appeared through the misting sky, the surging crowd let out a communal cry and joyful parents lifted their children high to catch the first glimpse of the Holy City. Coming closer, they passed wintering fields where the farmers – wearing brilliant turbans, red, yellow, blue, green – glowed like bright flowers in the subdued landscape.

As they neared the gates, a shiver moved through the swelling crowds, then a community murmur followed by a wave of sound rising like a low moan, as though one voice was calling in awe. The crowd parted on either side of the road, some dropping to their knees, others hunching low or sitting cross-legged. The old man sank to his knees, marveling how he had become part of this living throng.

Faces turned with radiant expectation toward a motorcar that appeared, top down. Each pilgrim bowed with their hands held at their heart and their eyes open in devotion toward an elderly man with a long white beard, dressed as the old man was, in a simple white *kurta* and turban, with a woolen shawl wrapped around his shoulders, his hands resting on a walking stick. Though the Holy Man sat, regal and still, in the back of the vehicle, His eyes moved rapidly toward the throng, first looking to one side of the road, then the other. Then the Master's glance pierced the old man's eyes and it was as though a sun had penetrated into the old man's soul, and lit a pause of eternity that left him trembling before he was pulled by the crowd through the gates of the Holy City.

The face and the eyes of the Master remained like a light within the old man. If he closed his eyes, He was there like a visionary fragrance that permeated his being with the essence of love. Dazed, flowing with the crowd, he let himself be guided to sit on a mat underneath a line of trees. A plate and cup were placed before him. Soon, two strong Sikh men carrying a large pot ladled *dal* and rice on his plate, and the young men following behind gave him a *chapati*, and filled his cup with water. The old man ate and drank in a cloud of wonderment, the eyes and face of the Holy Man appearing before his inner sight whenever he closed his eyes.

When the old man finished his meal, he followed those before him and washed his plate and spoon and bowl in a large sink. A man next to him asked, "Have you come for initiation?" The old man nodded his assent because he knew he wanted anything and everything that was offered by the Lord of this place. He followed the man and soon found himself outside the temple he had first glimpsed in the distance. After checking his belongings and shoes, he was led to sit in a row of men facing a low dais. Burnished by the sun, his clothes tattered and dusty, a shadow remnant of his past privileged life, the old man sighed and knew he had found what he had been seeking. Whenever the old man closed his eyes, a light storm lit up his inner world and a rise of joy danced through his body, erasing all traces of fatigue as his heart expanded with a flowering wildness of hope.

"I have heard wise men say that the beginning and the ending are the same. Now I know the dream of this place has been carried in my depths like a seed that seeks a ground where it can grow. I left my home in spite of fear and a lifetime of habit. A great longing released me from a home that had both nurtured and imprisoned me toward something I could not imagine but only felt a hunger for. And now, it is as though this place has always been the home I have been seeking."

The old man's thoughts flew back to the day he left his ancestral home and set out on the pilgrimage that led him to this place and this moment, to the now that blossomed within his being as a most beautiful flower of his soul on the sacred ground of the Holy City.

SEASONS OF SEEKING

SPRING

As he sat in his place in the lines of men waiting for the Master to appear, the old man remembered the first morning of his pilgrimage. The memory of that day seemed as far away as another life, but it was only a few months ago. Although it now seemed like a story of someone else, it was a story that drew him to his memories because it was the story of the journey that had brought him to this place. Yes, he remembered the day he left his ancestral home.

It was early one morning when the old man rose from his devotions and knew exactly what he had to do. Instead of fine clothes, he put on his oldest white *kurta* and trousers, wrapped a white turban loosely on his head, and slipped into worn garden sandals. With quiet purpose, he gathered a change of clothes, socks, a sweater, underwear, a thin raincoat, umbrella, gloves, and all the rupees in his drawer into his warmest shawl and tied it securely.

It would be hours before the household missed him, so he chose less traveled roads that took him into the countryside. "They will not find me even if they look for me," he reassured himself as he bowed to a wandering *sadhu*. Fear quavered in his heart, but as the morning passed, he discovered no one paid attention to him. Without his car and driver, he was just another old man on the road.

As he relaxed, he felt the earth rough beneath his feet. Bicycles and carts stirred swirls of dust as they passed him on the road. Crows shifted like shadows in the newly leafed trees, cawing their raucous squawks, while vultures hovered slowly in the deeper sky. Horned cattle grazed in the fields with dainty white birds riding on their backs, the cattle moaning a lower octave in the symphony of life. Farmers walked behind massive bullocks as they ploughed the fields. They moved slowly, repeating generations of tradition in a heritage of poverty. Although the farmers were worn lean by strenuous work, the old man respected the value of their labor that provided food for the peoples of his country.

The old man warmed shyly to the life around him as he walked past a farmhouse where an elderly grandfather sitting in the sun proudly showed him his beloved grandchild sleeping in his lap. Further along, he caught a glimpse of a young man standing in a courtyard pouring a jug of water over his head as he washed his long black hair. In the villages, he delighted in the beauty of young girls walking to school in navy uniforms brightened by crisp white blouses, their gleaming braids swinging in time with their laughter. Young boys swaggered near them in rough and tumble groups trying to attract their attention. As he passed ragged infants playing in the dust in front of tin and cardboard shacks near construction sites, he admired their mothers carrying jugs of water and bundles of brush for their cooking fires, and felt a tug of sadness in his heart. After months of solitary grieving, he was both charmed and sorrowed by the life of the people, for so few enjoyed happiness or ease in their harsh struggle for survival. As a government official, he had accomplished little to improve the lives of the poor, even though he had dreamed of doing so as a young man.

During the heat of the day, as he rested by a stream, a family generously shared their *chapatis* and *dal* with him. After thanking them, he was glad to close his eyes and doze beneath a tree. As he slept, a dream of knowing was gifted to him, and he knew that the remainder of his life must be devoted to the journey of his soul. He gave thanks for the strength that had enabled him to leave his ancestral home, and spoke aloud, arms wide before the sky, tears gathering in his eyes. "Lord, lead me to you. I walk only toward you."

When he folded his blanket, he noticed a branch under the tree, tested it for a cane, and was pleased, so he carried it in his right hand, the blanket draped over his shoulders, and the shawl bundle tied round his waist. As the old man walked through farmlands during the afternoon, he absorbed the beauty of the shining leaves and spring-green grasses gleaming in the rays of the lowering sun, and sighed with an ease he had not felt for a long time.

As evening advanced, he found himself near a shepherd gathering his goats in a flurry of clanking bells and bleats. The young man waved to the old man to join him by his fire before night settled on the land. Later, sheltering under a bush, inhaling the odors of goats mingled with scents of ripening blossoms and crushed green grasses, the old man lay for hours watching the stars move their patterns across the night sky. After a time, the strange beauty of his presence in the meadow surrendered to his fatigue and carried him into a deep sleep.

In the early morning, birdsong roused him before the dawn, and the young shepherd, all tousled black hair and rumpled clothes, bowed his *namasté* with a friendly smile as he welcomed the old man to his morning fire. And so the old man and the young man hunched together in the pastel dawn, silent, wrapped in shawls, their eyes full of the sunrise morning as they sipped warm, tangy, goat milk. The old man's fragile joy struggled against the weight of his recent grief until his heart opened in thanksgiving. He had waited all his life for a moment like this.

"All this the Lord is giving me," the old man said as he opened to his pilgrimage on his second day away from home. As he walked, he offered friendly greetings to the village folk, farmers, and children, and occasionally joined other travelers to enjoy their company for a while. He also savored his solitude. Often tears ran down his cheeks, blending the joy of his new life with nostalgia for the life he had left behind.

As he merged into the dust and clamor of the road, he found pleasure in simplicity. He purchased a bowl, cup, knife, and spoon from a shop so that he could buy fruits and vegetables from the farmers and markets. He enjoyed occasional cups of *chai* from the roadside *chai wallas,* fresh milk from farms, or water from village wells. Sometimes he shared meals with other travelers or ate in rustic roadside cafés. Whenever he found a stream, he bathed and then waited for his clothes to dry on bushes during the heat of the day. When he slept on the ground, feeling the earth strong beneath him, he wondered how he could have lived his seventy-three years without such simple joys. The old man marveled at his natural enjoyment of the wandering life, and could think of no reason to return to his ancestral home.

He found himself observing babies and young children with fascination, something he had never taken the time to do with his son or the servants' children. He discovered children were natural, intelligent, and curious about everything around them. The babies looked at him with concentration, with a knowing light that connected the old man to a greater soul love. He contemplated the unknown place of soul crossings, where the newborn enter into this world as the dying depart, and he sought for lingering soul truth in their bright, young eyes. With compassion born of his own difficult departure from his ancestral home, he realized that babies also leave their mothers' wombs to enter a new cycle of life. They too, knew when it was time to leave. He acknowledged that babies endure struggle and pain as they birth into the world. With acceptance that his departure from his home after months of conflict and struggle was the next cycle of his destiny, the old man turned once more to his pilgrimage, thankful for the leaving of one life for the seeking of another.

As the old man slowed into the pace of life on the road, into observing nature and interacting with the people, he opened to new perceptions. He was seeing, noticing, hearing, listening, and feeling with fresh clarity. When he observed a flower, he was present with its colors, textures, patterns, and geometry, and in awe of the flower's beauty, but also aware of its greater cycle. He enjoyed imagining a flower's journey from seed hibernation in dark earth to its powerful growth in response to warmth, light, and moisture. He followed its rise in his mind to its flowering before releasing the promise of new life in seed flight as it offered its petals and leaves as nourishment for new growth. He also became aware of the myriad tiny lives of the flying, fluttering, scattering, creeping, crawling, buzzing insects and creatures, understanding how each species is an essential part of nature.

Whenever rain fell, he watched the water rise in the streams and fill the irrigation ditches before spreading into the farmers' fields to nourish the crops. The old man noticed how birds shadowed patterns against the sky as the rush of their wings fluttered in his ears. He witnessed the spring birthing of calves and their tottering first steps accompanied by helpless bleating, and admired the calm nurturing of their mothers toward their newborn.

"So busy was my life," he reminisced, "I never had time to watch and learn and listen to the life around me." And so as time passed, a quiet happiness spread through him as he began to feel a part of the world around him. "I belong again," he sighed with the quiet pleasure that had always been his way.

"In my old life with my family, I performed with manners based on privilege and position, but rarely did my heart stir in excitement, passion, or joy. I never felt the heart sorrow of others because I would not let myself feel my own. I never looked deeply into other's eyes to see the light of their soul because I could not see my own soul. This wandering life is more real to me than the life I lived in my ancestral home," the old man realized as he trembled with a soul awakening that welcomed the tears gathering in his eyes and the aching in his heart.

"This ache and this longing is more true than my dedication to duty and all my years of service. I was a sleepwalker and to think that I believed that I was the most fortunate of all people. To think, I was afraid of death when I was already dead to life. Oh the foolishness of it all!"

After many months of grieving his wife's passing, when the love that had supported him through his life had vanished, the old man felt like he was falling into himself. But this self was not a self he knew, because he had never been alone before. His aged parents had passed the year before his wife's death, and were no longer there to offer their protection, wisdom, and noble hospitality. His wife was not there to charm and enchant him with her constant loving attention as she managed their household with skillful grace. His servants, who had been with him since childhood, were not there to greet him with tea in the morning and take care of all his needs.

The self he discovered after his wife's death was not a self he was comfortable with. This self did not know how to reach out and ask for things. This self did not know how to relate to his busy son and his wife who now managed the household with a rushed efficiency that lacked the warmth and ease he was accustomed to. This self only knew how to grieve and long for what was past. This self did not know how to make a new beginning. And so he retreated through a winter of isolation, until the falling into grief landed him in the soil of all loss, all longings, and he discovered an ember long forgotten, the ember of his soul longing.

It was this soul longing that enabled the old man to imagine a new life, and a departure of freedom to seek and find a spiritual teacher, and the path to his own death. Yet this longing still held the fear that he would be refused. And so, the old man's departure from his ancestral home was planned secretly. He would not, could not, tell his family that he wanted to leave. Instead he distanced himself because he feared discovery. He knew he could not stand up to them if they begged him to stay, and so he kept silent, and that silence carried the price of shame.

From one point of view, it seemed simple. He had served his family, completed his work in the world, and in keeping with the religious traditions of his upbringing, he was ready for the journey of his soul. The longing to search for a teacher had been born of soul searching and conflicts that had torn the fabric of his life apart. In the end there was no choice. When leaving became the only possible truth, he set himself free.

His departure was a death to all he knew and all that he had been. His passion to seek a spiritual teacher to guide him toward his death burned so strongly that it freed him from clinging to habit, comfort, and safety. The old man left the home that had been his haven of comfort and love all his life, and walked into India, into seeking and into trust.

The memory of his painful internal passage toward his physical departure inhabited him like an unwelcome guest, but he knew if he had not suffered with such intensity he would never have come to his freedom. Even with her death, his wife had gifted him with the grief that had stirred his soul awakening. A soaring love for her lightened his step and strengthened him. He must prove worthy of the love that had been given him during his life. He must find a way to enter into the greater soul love that the saints write about in their poems, the *shabd* songs and the *bhajans* of his mother country, the songs celebrating the spiritual passion of the mystics.

Later that day, as he rested under a canopy of leaves filtering the afternoon sun, the old man emerged from a dream of his son's return from his business trip. Images of his son's shock to find his father gone flickered in the old man's mind, but in his dream he could do nothing to ease his son's pain. He also knew he could not return. His time with his family was complete, and yet the tug of affection, rituals, duties, and familiar surroundings still held a place in his heart.

Whenever questions, guilt, or loss surged in his mind, he reasoned, "They would have to let me go when I die, so they might as well let me go now."

The memories of his departure after months of grief and conflict still haunted the old man. As often as he tried to push the memories away, they returned, demanding attention. He wanted to find a way to make peace with his past and release the burden of guilt. "Perhaps the only way to forget is to allow the memories to surface as I open to this new life," he decided, and so the old man wove past memories into the footsteps of his pilgrimage.

The old man had been so well cared for during his life that he had not recognized the retreat of love during his long winter of grief because the loss of his beloved wife, Anjali, shadowed all losses. Then one day, instead of dreaming her face into his heart and mind and submerging into longing for what once was, the old man woke to the world around him and realized the love that had embraced him all his life was no longer there.

The old man had always been loved: adored as a child, honored as a student and businessman, respected as the head of the family, looked up to as a community leader, cherished by his parents, wife and son. He always imagined he would remain the honored head of the family, a kind patriarch in his elder years, but how quickly he had lost his place during his months of mourning. He realized then that most of his life had been a blessing of love from his parents and his wife. With them gone – his grandchildren away at school; trusted servants retired; old school friends passed on, ill or absent; his son away on business trips – his role as gracious host to friends and guests, neighbors and supplicants had vanished, leaving him without purpose.

He had been born in the family compound, the old *haveli*, a three-story square of spacious rooms surrounding a courtyard garden. His favorite place to sit in the garden had always been the bench near the *neem* tree that dispensed the twigs he cleaned his teeth with while sitting in the shade during the heat of summer or wrapped in shawls in the winter months, and yet he never went there anymore. The *haveli* had always been his home, and even though he still lived there, it no longer felt like his home. How had he become a stranger in his own home?

The rooms that he and his wife had shared in the *haveli* felt like a shrine after her passing. Her dear essence had been absorbed into the walls, the carpets, and the old wooden bed they had slept in from the day they were married – so shy they were when they crept beneath the linens. When Mina, his daughter-in-law, painted their rooms when he had visited his wife's family after her death, he had returned alone to the rooms that once had great meaning for him to find that they too contained the painful reality of loss. Only the pictures of his wife glowed out of the freshly painted walls, like portals into beloved memories.

During his absence Mina had also retired his trusted servants who had been with him for most of the years of his marriage. When he discovered their departure, the old man had cried silently in the night, missing their remembering of their years together, as well as their kind attention to his needs. His hands shook when he placed the letters and gifts in his son's hands to send to them.

"Papa *Ji*," his son had said in defense of his wife. "Please understand. Mina wants to make the house bright and fresh. This is her household now. She wants her own servants."

The old man said nothing. He excused his daughter-in-law, imagining she wanted to please him. He tried his best to accept her enthusiasm for modernizing their ancestral home, yet his sense of displacement increased. Life had moved on without him during his months of bereavement, and he did not know how to accept his daughter-in-law as the center of the family. At first Mina had served him well, or so it seemed, suggesting that he rest, excusing his absence at meals, telling the children to leave him in peace, protecting him from guests and visitors. When he realized she had separated him from the family, the time he spent in his rooms became a penance rather than the peaceful pleasure he had always enjoyed.

"I don't feel comfortable in my own home anymore. I am irritable and restless and I don't like myself this way. I know what is upsetting me but I feel helpless, like there is nothing I can do to change things," the old man muttered to himself.

He and Anjali had been kind to Mina when she arrived a stranger in their home, a new wife away from her family, barely knowing her husband. Anjali taught her the secrets of household management, helped her with pregnancy and birthing, never asking her to work too long or too hard. He and his wife rejoiced that their son was happy with his wife and that two healthy sons had been born to the family. She had been a good daughter-in-law all these years, and he could understand her passion to make the home her own, but he could not accept the loss of his position in the family.

The old man and his wife had honored their parents through their old age, always including them and deferring decisions to their wisdom and experience. He could never imagine painting their rooms without consulting them, or sending away their servants. The old man knew times were changing, and that tradition was not as strong, but no matter how he tried to accept Mina's changes, he could not release the pain in his heart or the awkwardness of displacement, and so he kept to himself, choosing further separation.

"Her time has come," and who am I to deny that?" he reasoned whenever arguments circled in his mind. "What good would it do to complain? The painting is done. My servants are gone. There is nothing I can do."

The changes continued. The courtyard that had been a source of delight all his life no longer contained the kitchen garden with the treasured medicinal herbs nurtured by his wife's love of healing plants. It had diminished into a pattern of cement paths, confined pots, and rows of militant plants doing their best to look brave. It was no longer the vibrant hub of family life where children played and cups of tea were shared with loved ones while servants chattered as they cut vegetables, hung clothes to dry, mended clothes, or cleaned pots. The benches were gone. The *neem* tree had been cut down. There was nowhere for anyone to choose a favorite place in the sun on a cold winter day, or enjoy the breezes and the shade in the heat of summer.

Beyond the compound, the trees along the drive from his grandfather's time had been cut down to make room for a parking lot, and stone pillars supported a decorative metal gate. It was all for show now, not for living. Everywhere around him, all that he had cherished was disappearing. As he could not bear to look upon the garden, he kept the curtains pulled and retreated further into grief, loss and pain.

The grandchildren had been sent away to school, so their bright faces disappeared too, even though their laughter and love echoed in his heart's memories. He longed for their company, but when they returned for holidays they had new friends and new interests. They rarely stepped inside his room for anything other than a brief hello before they dashed away. He missed the boys, Pani and Jani, and mourned that they no longer wanted to rub his legs or beg for stories about his life.

His own dear son, Rajiv, was traveling, earning more, and spending more, so he was always busy. There was such a flurry of preparation and excitement when he returned. His good son always stopped in, but it seemed he did all the talking now, even answering his own questions.

"Papa *Ji*, you look good. They are taking good care of you, yes? Must run, so many things to do. Will stop by later. Are you comfortable? Yes?"

Dressed in silk *kurtas* and fine sandals, Rajiv rushed his goodnights before leaving for social events, and often did not say goodbye when he left for his next business trip, and the old man was left to wonder, "What has become of my loving son?"

He couldn't remember when he had lost the right of approval for expenditures and improvements and repairs. The beautiful *Rajasthani* antiques of his childhood had been replaced with modern furniture, and there was continuous disturbance with painting, carpentry, and the fittings of carpets and curtains. The house was always busy: Mina calling out orders, the servants running, the doorbell ringing, workers hammering and carrying things about. It seemed that all he loved and enjoyed had vanished from his life.

At first, he wanted to feel a part of the family and belong again, but he did not know what to do. All his life his family and servants had cared for him. "They knew what I needed more than I did," the old man remembered, keenly aware the traditions and habits of his life had made him passive.

And then one day, stronger words rose within him with a fierceness that shocked him. "I can't wait to die hiding in my rooms, but where would I go?"

Once he had asked the question, it simmered beneath the surface of his life, creating a current of restlessness that disturbed his ground of being. Other questions surfaced. "What should I do with the rest of my life? How should I prepare for my departure from this world? How can I make best use of the time I have left?"

Questioning led him toward a seeking that carried him into a deeper longing for spiritual love and guidance. Searching within himself, he discovered a passionate force that sought to break free from his hibernation of grief and passive acceptance.

At first he could not face the truth of his feelings. He was ashamed of the desire that would take him away from his ancestral home and his family, but he could not stop himself from imagining his departure.

"If I told them I wanted to leave, they would think they had done something wrong. They would insist on taking care of me, and I know I would give in," he argued. "I have money. I could go anywhere, but there is nowhere I want to go. It is better I follow the traditions of my people and go on a pilgrimage."

The old man's plans were seasoned with fear. As his longing to seek a spiritual teacher grew stronger, so did his arguments. Conversations filled his mind, keeping him up through the nights.

He imagined his family pleading, "Papa, you are not strong enough to go on pilgrimage." "Grand *Ji*, don't go. We need you here." "Papa, we're here to take care of you. How can you leave?"

He also imagined their inner thoughts. "What would people say?" "He is going to pass soon, so it's better he stays at home." "He has not been the same since his wife died." "He isn't strong enough for a pilgrimage. Look at how he just lies around all day."

The old man was not used to keeping secrets and felt shame at his longing to leave his family. He feared he would be found out, so he began to make his excuses to avoid their company, telling them he was too tired to come to meals. He did not feel strong enough to face opposition, and his desire was too passionate to accept compromise. The urge for solitude felt strange. He had never wanted to be alone before. Raging thoughts and passionate feelings demanded his attention, urging him toward the unknown within himself.

"I have become a child again," he cried, alarmed at his trembling weakness during long nights of wavering confusion. The more he faced the reality of death and the fear that he had not prepared himself, the stronger the desire to leave his home and seek spiritual refuge with a teacher surged within him. When he felt he would break with the strain, something let go within him, and the old man accepted that the journey to his death was his own. With this change of attitude, rebellion surfaced again.

The old man raged. "Why should I ask permission? In India it is accepted that an elder can retire into a spiritual life."

As the old man was not used to asserting his will, he found it difficult to control the passionate conflicts that burst forth and then had to be subdued within his own being. As difficult as these emotions were, he felt like he had got in touch with some essential part of himself that he had lost in his childhood. Strong as family ties were, they were not strong enough to hold him back from his soul.

The old man weathered these storms of rebellion until the confusion and conflicts settled into a calmer knowing. He also knew he must accept that seeking in the sunset of his life might not necessarily lead to finding a teacher before his passing.

"The seeking will be enough," he promised himself. "Let the Lord Himself find me, as I do not know how to find Him." And so it was that the old man walked away from his home without farewells, leaving no explanation, and it was as if he had died to his family and they had died to him.

He remembered his studious childhood and how one desk had replaced another during his life as an engineer and community leader. Although he had lived a privileged life as a landowner, he had shed all the trappings of his caste when he left home. As a seeker and a homeless wanderer, he no longer wanted anyone to defer to him or honor him. "When I meet my death, caste will mean nothing, so it is best I leave it behind now."

"I don't miss the house or my family. I don't long for the comforts of my bed or my bath. I don't miss anything," he shouted to the cattle in the field, startling birds into flight, as his heart rejoiced at the freedom of his new life.

"It is my time now," he said as he gathered his things. "I have loved and served my family, and now it is time to seek and know God."

Although a feeling of sadness accompanied this remembrance of the time before his departure, the old man also felt relief that he had been able to approach the memory without being lost in deeper currents of grief and conflict. Relieved to leave the past behind, he gave thanks for the strength that enabled him to find his own way.

The old man drew water from a nearby well and continued his wandering. Whenever memories surfaced, he allowed the images and feelings to flow through him and be released. Sometimes he honored the sacrifices his family made on his behalf, and at other times he felt the sorrow of lost opportunities and wasted time. More often, the old man cherished the memories of the many fine days of his life, and offered thanks to those who had made his life pleasant and bountiful. His memories so inhabited his attention that he had barely noticed the landscapes or villages he was passing through, but after a time they faded and he opened once more to his soul journey.

"I could never have this freedom and this journey if I had not been able to leave my home and my family," the old man realized. "I cannot explain or understand my life. I was the way I was. I loved my family and fulfilled my duties the best I could, even though I see now that I could have been a better person. I must let the past go and live my new life. I am thankful it is not too late to seek the path of my soul."

SUMMER

As spring blossomed toward the burning heat of summer, the old man wandered as though it did not matter in what direction he went: north, east, south, or west. This aimless wandering led him to discover aspects of himself he had never noticed before: how curiosity led him in one direction, how fear or a sense of resistance made him hesitate and then choose another direction, or how he followed others who told him about some teacher or temple. He was drawn by laughter around campfires and experienced compassion when he witnessed the suffering of others. Without expectation, duty or tradition limiting him, he began to feel his emotions, feelings, responses, reactions, and interpretations, as something wondrous. He delighted in following his impulses to see where they would lead.

"If I am seeking," the old man mused, "then what I am seeking must also be seeking me. I am not only seeking. I am being found." This thought amused him so much that he burst out laughing. Birds scattered in the bushes nearby, and he felt the beat of their wings as they flew past his head. "Even this is a sign I am on the right path," he thought.

After a time, this way of wandering became natural, slowly evolving into spontaneous knowing as though he had an internal pendulum. It was rare that the old man did not know which way to go, but when he could not decide, he learned to wait until he did know, or until he was invited by some sign, a person, or a fluttering of the wind in the trees that spoke to his heart.

And then there was the day when he could not choose. Three paths lay before him. If he stepped forward onto one, it produced a sense of dread or resistance, and he had to backtrack into the crossroads and sit on a stone, his heart beating. If he tried another path, his body would not move. He could not take a step forward.

"What is this?" he asked, but there was no answer.

The sun rose in the sky but still he could not proceed, and there were no other travelers to ease him on his way. He tried to return the way he came, but the same thing happened. Something was keeping him in this place. From time to time, he would try a path, but he was unable to choose one that felt right to his more finely tuned senses.

At high noon, the old man surrendered with a laugh and let go of the tension and uncertainty that had haunted his morning, saying, "So this is my place? All right, I will stay here until I know which path to take." Having made this decision, he stretched out under a tree, curled up as best he could on the uneven surface, and settled into rest.

The old man woke as the lowering sun glowed through soft clouds drifting slowly overhead. He immediately sat up, eager to see what direction he should take, but then he heard bells, singing and chanting accompanied by the stamping of feet and howling laughter. The old man rubbed his eyes as he wondered what was coming toward him. Then on the middle path, a wild *sadhu* appeared, singing and dancing to the tune of hundreds of bells that were tied to his robes and hung around his neck.

The first thought that crossed the old man's mind was, "I never thought of dancing down a path," and then he stood up and bowed his "*Namasté*." The *sadhu* was dressed in faded, dusty ochre robes. His matted hair hung in locks around his shoulders where it joined chains, necklaces of bells, and pendants that swung as one every time he leapt or circled during his dancing walk. Instead of standing still to return the bow, the *sadhu* spun and laughed and stamped his feet before he roared his greeting to the song of bells, "*Namasté*. I am glad to know you obeyed instructions and waited for me."

"Waited for you? Was that what I was doing?"

"Of course, why else are you here?"

"I couldn't go forward. Every time I stepped on a path, the path said, 'No!'"

"Of course, every path has a 'Yes' or a 'No.' I am glad to know you now know!" The *sadhu* laughed and spun and stamped with glee. "And now it is time to follow me."

The *sadhu* gestured to the old man to follow him along the middle path, and the old man gathered his things and walked behind him.

"It is time for you to learn how to dance. Enjoy yourself. Have a little fun," the *sadhu* encouraged the old man, pushing him, and then taking his hand to spin him around. As the evening encroached on the lingering early summer day, the two men danced and laughed to the tune of bells, and shouted wild songs along the dusty path.

The old man enjoyed their playful progress, but after a time he felt fatigued. Fighting against a bodily heaviness, he continued without complaint because he was enchanted with this new companion, and did not want to show his weakness. He admired the seemingly endless energy of the *sadhu* and wished he could dance as lightly.

Just as darkness dimmed the rocky landscape into indistinct, luminous shapes, the *sadhu* turned into a passage between two massive boulders that opened into a clearing shadowed by a cliff. Quietly chanting, the *sadhu* slowed his ecstatic dance to enter a cave, light a candle, and motion for the old man to follow and sit on a stone shelf. The old man watched as the *sadhu* set the fire, and hung a pot of water over the flames.

When the *sadhu* turned to look fully at the old man, his heart skipped a beat from the force of energy radiating from his wild companion. Then the *sadhu* laughed and the old man joined in the laughter with relief. Later, they shared tea and a strong, nourishing soup of greens and roots. The old man alternately stared into the fire and then at the radiant laughing face of his companion who sang one *bhajan* after another, uncertain which was the most potent warmth. After a time, the old man felt drowsy and lay on his mat beside the fire. He fell asleep to the songs and laughter that seemed to echo in his dreams throughout the night.

As the morning light stirred his awakening, the old man heard chattering and saw monkeys scrambling at the entrance of the cave. Dozens of them perched on boulders, hung from branches or swung in the trees in the clearing. One baby monkey was nestled in the *sadhu's* lap while the mother sat nearby, watching their play.

"Very good, you are awake," said the *sadhu.* "The monkeys are my companions but they can be dangerous. Feed them these bananas so they know you are a friend. They are the best protectors, not that there is anything I need to be protected from." Then he howled with laughter as if this was the funniest thought in the world. The old man peeled the bananas and the monkeys gathered around, seeming to chatter and laugh and play like the *sadhu* as they took the bananas, peeled them, and ate them with relish.

Later, after the old man had completed his morning ablutions at a nearby stream, he returned to the cave and saw that the *sadhu* had prepared an herbal tea and cut mango fruit for breakfast. The monkeys were eating the skins and chattering and grooming themselves, and the old man gently found a place amongst them.

"I can see you are new to this seeking on the paths and roads of India," the *sadhu* giggled. "Quite obvious. So serious you are. And what is your excuse for this wandering?"

"My wife died," the old man said sadly. The *sadhu* immediately leapt up, laughing and holding his stomach as if he had just heard the funniest joke in the world.

"Oh, your look, it's killing me," the *sadhu* continued, howling, with tears running down his face. "And what else made you leave your dear home?"

"Well, my daughter-in-law sent my old servants away, sold all the furniture that had been in the family for generations, painted my rooms, and I felt I didn't belong anymore...." The old man stopped speaking because the *sadhu* was acting crazier and crazier, and all the old man could do was watch in astonishment at the display. The monkeys joined in the madness and leapt around the cave, making faces and shrieking with laughter.

After a time, the *sadhu* managed to stop his howling and dancing and return to his seat. Rubbing his eyes, he exclaimed, "Oh, what a wonderful gift to have you here! Oh, what a treat! You just don't get how the divine Lord of the Universe arranged it so perfectly to set you free for this journey. I am sure you had to make it such a problem, such a decision, such a secret, such an escape. Am I right?" The *sadhu* saw the look on the old man's face and leapt up again, howling and laughing and dancing with monkeys. "Enough of your story," he said between gasps of glee. "If I hear any more, I will die of laughter."

The *sadhu* sat down and the monkeys crowded around him as he fed them mangos and bananas. The old man watched in amazement, feeling like he had entered a mad world where everything was upside down.

The *sadhu* turned to the old man, this time with an even more piercing eye and questioned, "And where are you going, old man?"

Almost afraid to answer, the old man said quietly, "I want to find a teacher to help me open to my spiritual life. I know I am going to die soon and I want to prepare for my passing." He noticed the *sadhu* was listening intently, and so he continued.

"I feel this strong pull inside, like I have to look for something. I don't exactly know what yet, but it feels good to have left my home. And yes, I did suffer grief, loss, conflict, confusion, guilt and more. They were my companions for far too long. How did you ever get to be so happy?"

The *sadhu* replied. "Happy crazy, you mean. Insanely happy, you mean. Mad ecstasy, you mean. I just see life as funny, like someone is playing a big joke. I am always laughing. I wake up giggling. You want to be more yourself? Then keep going on your pilgrimage, and I am sure you will find out what that is. For me this is it," he said as he gestured expansively at his cave and all the monkeys. "At least it is right now. I am sure it could change anytime if the Lord of Creation wanted something new from me. Right now this dancing, laughing, giggling, crazy *sadhu* is what pleases Him. So, yes, I am happy if the Great Lord is happy."

The *sadhu* looked at the old man carefully for a moment, fixing him with his bright eyes and joyful face, before exclaiming, "All seekers want to find God, and they walk, and look, and search, but very few want to know God."

"That is what I want," replied the old man quietly. "I want to know God."

"Then you must know God within yourself. If you are searching for a teacher, find one who can show you the path within. And then if you want to go even further, become one with God."

The old man could think of no reply, and he needed time to reflect, and so he turned to the monkey crawling over his back and fed him a banana.

After a time, he turned to the *sadhu* and asked, "This cave is your home?"

"Yes, but I come and go," the *sadhu* replied. "I go on pilgrimages and visit temples. When I am here, I seem to receive instructions in many different ways, and like a good disciple of the God of the Universe, I pay attention to them. Sometimes they are impulses, or I wake from a dream with an image or direction. Sometimes it is just a feeling, like this morning when I sensed someone was coming. That was very real to me, and so I came to greet you. Stay as long as you like, and go when you are ready, but don't expect me to teach you or anything. Here you can be yourself, so it is a good time to discover more of who you are."

For a few days, the two men shared their daily routines. The old man explored, collected fruit, and helped tidy the cave and clearing. He walked every morning to a nearby stream where he bathed, washed clothes, and lay in the sun. When he returned, he carried water back to the cave, and helped prepare their simple meals or play with the monkeys. Mostly he watched and felt and learned by seeing and hearing and touching. He felt like a child again, all enthusiasm, all awake, all alive.

At night, as the old man and the *sadhu* sat around the fire, the monkeys scrambled onto their laps, hung on their shoulders, and begged for treats while the *sadhu* told stories of gurus and swamis, quoted teachings, and sang the holy poems of the saints. The *sadhu* did not belong to any religion or path, and did not have a spiritual master, but it was clear he had been blessed by divine grace and was completely, uniquely, and happily, himself. The old man watched the *sadhu* light candles, ring bells, and chant before his collection of holy objects gathered on his pilgrimages, but he did not join in the rituals.

"Sometimes when I go on the road," the *sadhu* explained, "I listen and learn from gurus and holy men, but I have not found my own guru as some have. There is an absence of what that might be like, but there is also the presence of the divine, so I continue with my practices and meditation. I accept my *dharma* is to remain in loving presence, and be of service to all who come before me. So you see, I am content because I trust the guidance I receive from my inner communion. If I am meant to find my guru in this life, then I will find him. My life seems to be a combination of seeking and being content with what I have, and I can't complain about that!"

"I am learning much from you," the old man said gratefully.

"I am only a companion on the path, dear friend, nothing more, and this time together is good for both of us. I know you are leaving soon, and I bless you and your journey."

"Thank you. I do need to move on, but I wasn't sure how to let you know," the old man explained with some embarrassment.

The *sadhu* howled with laughter before he could speak. "Don't play those games you played with your family with me, dear friend. Just be honest. Wherever you go, say what you need and want, share your feelings, and move on when you are ready. Hiding your feelings will only create problems, and that would not be good for anyone. Hmmm, I just gave you a lesson. Imagine that! I knew you were ready to go, and was fine with it of course. I wouldn't be a good *sadhu* if I couldn't let go and enjoy my solitude, would I? Don't take care of me. Take care of yourself," the *sadhu* shouted as he jumped up, spun around and let out peals of laughter. The old man found this irresistible and joined the merry dance.

And so the next day, the old man gathered his

things, bowed a respectful *"Namasté,"* and set out on his path of 'Yes.'

"Perhaps today is the day," he shouted to the sky. "Perhaps today is the day."

As summer advanced, the old man wandered the paths and roads of India with a new awareness that his outer journey contained an inner journey of equal effort. The long hours of walking and resting provided solitude for prayer, meditation, and inquiry. His journeys led him to temples, mosques, caves, churches, and forests where he met and spoke with spiritual travelers and teachers of all castes and creeds. He bathed in the Ganges, purified himself in holy tanks, and was given blessings, but nowhere did he feel the thrill of recognition signaling that he had found what he was seeking. He knew death waited for him, but because seeking for a true teacher was his only goal, his life felt rich for now he was free to find his own way.

The sun's burning intensified and the old man walked in the morning and in the shade of evening when the sun was hidden behind the mountains. During midday, he sheltered under trees, behind buildings, by cool streams, and in caves. He had never been exposed to summer's burning before, but because the heat had come on slowly, he had adjusted. Like everyone around him, he longed for monsoon, for rain, for cool, and yet as the sun's fire penetrated into his bones, he felt it purified him.

Sometimes the old man crept down into the shade of ditches and dug into the soft, moist earth to wait out the intense hours of burning sun. There, in a grave of his own digging, he discovered the mysterious clicking and rustling of tiny insects, the winding traceries of cold worms, the feel of stones and dank earth against his skin, and the branching and weaving of roots. These spoke to him of the worlds that nourish the living and feed off the dead.

He tried to imagine his bones buried in the earth and his flesh as an offering of food for insects and worms. It felt strange to envision that his body – which had been with him from plump babyhood through the strength of manhood to this spare, weakening, aged frame – would no longer exist. In his family, dead bodies were burned so they did not suffer the degradation of decomposition, and yet the image of his body and his bones becoming food for the earth seemed at that moment preferable to the fire.

"There is something restful about lying in the earth," he reasoned. "Either way, my body will be left behind." He inhaled the odors of pungent humus and bitter roots, and crumbled moist earth on his face and body. As he lay in the earth, he held cool stones in his hands, grateful for respite from the burning sun. "But when my body is dead, where will my soul go?"

Sometimes, he floated in shallow streams to blend with reeds and grasses in the flowing currents. His immersion in the symphony of water drowned all sounds except the rustling of pebbles and stones. The moving embrace of ripples and waves caressed and cooled him as he held on to boulders or sheltered against the banks so he would not be carried away.

Whenever the old man surrendered to the water, he felt the edges of his body disappear and become one with moving, changing water. He imagined his ashes floating, and then swirling away in the currents to settle among the stones. In the water, the sense of his imminent dissolution merged together with his longing for a teacher, as though the nearness of death increased the urgency of his seeking, until it felt like a pain or a hunger that could only be satisfied by something that was beyond dissolution. There was a knowing in him that imagined an infinite realm beyond all that he knew was possible.

"It is not that I want to live forever. It is that when I die, I want to follow my soul to my true home," he spoke out loud, feeling the strangeness of his voice joining the bubbling currents, before he returned to his silent inner thoughts.

"The mystics speak of the ocean of love, but how can I find my way there? If I imagine my soul as a stream, I will have to flow into the great ocean of soul," he mused. "All souls must return to their source," he pondered. "They also say that we are pulled by our attachments to return life after life. How do I release the attachments that inhabit my mind like stories that never end?"

For a time, the old man wandered through desolate landscapes: dry, scrub hills with spare trees that overlooked shallow, placid streams, and burning stretches of sand strewn with pebbles, rocks and stone. Walking in the intense heat tested his endurance, but he learned to pace himself, to slow into the rhythm and nature of a place until he felt a part of it. By paying attention, he discovered water when he needed it or a cool place to rest when he was tired. "I am walking in God," he thought one day. "He is already taking care of me."

One day, he discovered a river shadowed by large boulders where he found a cool, sheltered crevice in which to settle for a while. The boulders spoke to him. He leaned into their shade, listening to their eternity, feeling his cells slow to their stillness, and enjoying the cool touch of stone on his skin. Following animal tracks, and bird flight patterns, the old man found edible herbs, berries, and fruits in the dry lands, and if he needed to go without a meal, he did not mind.

At night, he climbed over the boulders to search for and then settle on a flat surface where he could lie on his back to ponder the vast array of brilliant stars in the formless deep night. The sky seemed vast and unknowable, but the giant boulders grounded him as he blended the singing of the stars and the moaning of slow, hard stone into one sound. On these nights, the old man did not sleep. His body pulsed, his cells rang, and a sound filled him that made him feel he had become part of the song of creation.

Some days later, he entered a sheltered shady valley of grasslands where a spring bubbled forth like the fountain of life. There, the lush grasses softly embraced him. Surprised flowers, startled butterflies and dedicated bees accompanied him as he waded deep in moist, water-logged meadows that grasped his sandals with a grip so strong he had to fight to free his feet. The feeling of the grasses felt luxurious after the spare deserts, dry hills, and stony places. He wandered, touching the tips of the grasses with his fingers, feeling their flexible coolness part before his strides, marveling in wonderment at the beauty of living sensation.

"I drove by these places all my life and never stopped to experience, to feel, to become part of them," the old man acknowledged as sorrow ached in his heart for the absence of connection in the blindness of his old life.

Whenever he found clay in a riverbed, he covered himself with the slick, slippery earth, enjoying the cool shivering before the sun's warmth cracked crazed, veined patterns over his body. Then he stretched onto hot rocks where their captured heat penetrated him to meet the baking from the sun. Immersion into heat satisfied him in a way he did not understand. He only knew that from time to time he must bake and burn so that a deeper calm would enter into him. When he cleansed the clay from his body, he felt as if he were releasing a crust of his old self, and he celebrated with the howling dancing he had learned from the *sadhu*.

"This body is coming alive even as it is dying," he thought, in awe at the sensations his elemental immersions awakened. "I am becoming part of nature, and like all things in nature, my body will die. All that is a part of me will become a part of nature, but where will my soul go? What is my soul? My soul cannot be this changeable mind? I feel there is something more, but I do not know what that is, but I seek it with all my heart."

The forests called him with their shaded mystery, but the old man had a dread of tigers, lions, and snakes, and so he beat his bowl with his spoon as he walked the mossy paths. The quiet receptivity of the trees, the gentle light that glowed through the swaying canopy of leaves overhead, the soft step of his feet on moss, the chatter of small animals, and the calls of birds enchanted him, but he always remained vigilant. He never slept in the forests unless he joined other travelers or wanderers around a fire.

Whenever this powerful primal fear left him for the safety of trust, the old man loved to sit under a tree, lean against the trunk, and listen to the life of its slow growing, the rising of sap, and the branching and leafing that mirrored the searching roots hidden beneath the earth. He would open into peace, as though the tree spoke in some unknown language of energy that both calmed and deepened his sense of presence. Eventually, his breath slowed and his mind settled into timelessness, as if he had became a part of the living forest. He loved the deepening quiet and how it helped him understand the meaning of the phrase so often heard during his life, 'As above so below,' and he matched the metaphor to his life. "Just like this tree, my seeking must be both earthward and soulward, but as yet I do not know how to do this. I only know that I feel its truth."

"Just like this tree, the deeper I search into my ground of being, the greater my expansion into my spiritual sky," he realized in a thrilling flash of understanding. He gathered his belongings, took his staff in his right hand and strode through the forest to seek and discover his path with renewed strength. "Perhaps today is the day I will find my teacher."

"It is good I am facing my fears," he decided, "as fear ruled me all my life and held me back." He remembered instances in his life when opportunities were offered to him, but fear prevented him from accepting them. How quickly he had bowed before that primal power. How quickly he had returned to his contracted life of duty, emotional distance, and comforting habits without understanding his loss.

It was difficult to reconcile the fear that had so often made him passive or resistant, with the childlike trust that seemed to be his natural state on his pilgrimage. At times, he wondered whether his sense of adventure was an illusion, or an enchantment of innocence that protected him during his wanderings. His joy carried him through discomfort, his wonderment transformed challenges into opportunities, and his awe recognized all as divine. And yet, fear still quivered in his belly.

A few days later, in a parched valley of rough, granulated sand and cracked earth, five mangy, barking dogs raged toward the old man with teeth bared. His knees gave way. He sank to the ground.

He closed his eyes and covered his ears to shut out their ferocious barking and escape the horror of their snapping teeth, and wild, hungry eyes. He did not know when the barking stopped or the dogs left, but when he opened his eyes, he was alone in a circle of footprints on the dusty ground, imprints of dark barking still steaming in his brain. He left that place quickly, his heart thumping in his chest, fearful they might return.

Fear became his companion. He could not forget the wild dogs. He constantly anticipated attack and became vigilant and defensive, always looking for danger, but after a time he could not bear the tension and returned to trust. "I must believe I am protected. I am on a sacred journey. I am seeking God." And so the old man opened to his adventure with renewed courage.

Once more a forest was before him. He waited a day, then two, for a companion to appear, but one did not. And so, the old man took a deep breath and entered the cathedral of ancient trees. He walked for sometime, opening to the light, the silence, and the living energy. Just as he felt a sense of peace and calm overcome his fear and open transparency to the beauty of the forest, a cobra rose in front of him, fanning its lethal head, eyes glittering. Without thinking, the old man hummed a childhood song as though a cellular memory activated the skills of the snake men who often visited his home. The cobra swayed in threatening potential and they remained locked in a magnetic connection until the bells of an approaching traveler broke the spell. The snake slid into the bushes and the old man fell to his knees. He was unable to speak when the traveler, a saffron-robed monk, approached quietly and stood before him. The old man could only bow with his hands to his heart.

The monk waited as the old man slowly recovered. When he was able to stand up, his knees were weak and his body shook. The monk beckoned him to follow, and as the old man walked along the path, he noticed that the trees, plants, bird life, insects, flowers, all the nature around him had brightened, as if lit from within. He marveled at his change in perception, but his mind refused to follow its usual paths of analysis.

"I have dropped into being," he felt rather than thought. "Facing death has made me more alive."

They stopped before a hut in a clearing, and the monk gestured for him to sit down on a blanket. The old man sank to the ground, suddenly weary, tears of relief lining his dusty face. They sat together for a time, sharing a natural silence. The old man could not speak, but he did not find this uncomfortable. It seemed as if he was empty, but he also felt awareness sensation, as his attention had fallen fully into each moment.

The monk boiled root vegetables gathered from the forest and offered soup to the old man. After they ate, he silently led the old man inside the hut and gestured toward a sleeping shelf where the old man fell immediately asleep.

The old man stayed in the encampment of the silent monk without measuring or knowing time. Light rose and darkness fell on the forest dwelling, and their shared silence felt all the more deep because of the background of the songs of birds, the skittering of small animals, and the rustle of leaves in the trees. The gentle movements of the monk and the old man as they silently shared cooking and cleaning shifted easily into long hours of stillness, reverie and meditation. The old man felt the shedding of layers of tension and he entered into a profound relaxation of both body and mind.

At night, before sleep overtook him, the old man's thoughts often returned to the day of the cobra and his arrival at the monk's encampment. "When the cobra hovered before me, something took over that was greater than my mind or my fear. I do not understand it, but I know I am changed."

Each day, as they walked slowly to the river for pure spring water, the monk showed the old man where to dig roots and pick herbs and leaves for the evening soup. The monk seemed to notice everything: a motionless bird on a branch, a hovering, iridescent dragonfly, or a small quivering animal hiding behind a bush. As the days passed, the old man felt his heart open, his steps become softly quiet, and his eyes more observant. The greatest change was the absence of fear. The forest now felt as safe and comfortable as his ancestral home.

And then one day, in a flash of inner knowledge, he finally understood his fear. "Whenever I am afraid,

I become paralyzed. I contract. All my life, I retreated to passivity and immobility to escape from stronger personalities. This was my nature, and I can see that it was both my weakness and my gift. It was a kind of surrender to the world that others shaped around me, a giving up of self to fit in with what others wanted and expected from me. The saints speak of surrender and I am not sure what that is, but perhaps one day my passive nature will become my strength."

Gradually, as the old man opened to the world of the forest, his imagined fears of encounters with tigers or snakes diminished. Eventually, all he felt was love for the beauty and life of the forest. For a time, he felt as though he were in heaven, like he wanted to stay there forever, and then another fear rose like a cobra inside him: the fear that he would have to leave. He saw and felt the fear like the presence of a malevolent apparition, and he knew the monk saw and felt it too, but the monk only smiled with love and understanding. Several days later, the monk gestured to him to gather plants for their evening soup, and the old man set off in the late afternoon, enjoying the light pouring through the leaves, the pattern of birdsong thriving through the air, the living dance of the trees in the breeze, and the touch of the grass on his feet.

When the old man arrived at the river, he sat for a time, listening to the varied rhythms of the water spiraling around the boulders as the coolness emanating from the spray refreshed him. After a time, he removed his clothes and submerged himself in the flowing waters before he lay on hot rocks in the full force of the summer sun. The flowing sounds, the heat of the sun, the cool spray, and the touch of stone carried him through silent stillness to a disappearing into luminous peace. As the afternoon light glowed golden, he rose to the surface of life with lazy reluctance and put on his clothes. Walking slowing, noticing the radiant details of the forest, he searched for herbs with tender attention until the roar of a wild beast shattered his enchantment. Immediately he froze, and then inexplicably he responded to a voice within him that said, "Turn and face your death." When he turned, the old man did not see his death. He saw a *sadhu* dressed as *Hanuman*, the monkey god, blowing a whistle that sounded like a roar. They laughed together, the old man and the monkey god, as they passed each other with a bow.

After this encounter, the old man knew that his presence in nature was an offering to trust that depended on his willingness to face life and death in each moment. "I cannot know the forest without accepting the risks. Oh, Lord, let me live in trust instead of fear," the old man begged as tears welled in his eyes. "If I am to journey in life, I must accept that death may come at any moment."

The old man walked hurriedly back to the camp in the gathering dusk, but when he arrived, he found that the hut had been leveled, his belongings placed neatly in a pile, and the monk gone. A piercing sense of loss found release in a cry that soared through the trees. The old man lay on the ground and wept. Later, he covered himself with his blanket and slept until the early dawn. He left the forest in the early morning, greatly changed.

"All my life I saw *sadhus*, yogis, monks, and holy men and women. I walked past them, drove by them, bowed to them in the temples, and fed them when they came to my home, but I never understood their wildness, their simplicity or their calm," he reminisced. "Although their appearance often frightened me, they also stirred my heart. I could not understand why they chose to live in the wilds and wander the streets of cities." Now the old man knew that each *sadhu* was on a unique journey, seeking soul connection and conscious participation in the mystery of life and death. These holy wanderers were willing to shed worldly comforts, so that their time and attention would be free to explore their inner world.

The old man experienced the wild beauty and sensuality of nature with the full intensity of awakened sight, touch, smell, and hearing. His body was sharing messages with his heart and mind, and creating a storm of change within him that transformed the way he viewed life, the world, and his own being. He was growing to love nature more than he had loved anything, as if nature were God, and yet it was still not enough. He knew he needed more than his passion for nature, and its harsher lessons of truth, pain and death. He was even more determined to find a teacher, a path, and a practice. "I am a part of nature, but nature is not enough. When my body dies it will return to nature. I want to follow my soul."

After he left the valley of the monk, the old man arrived in a more populated area where he encountered wanderers like himself. For a time, he walked with companions, and his days were filled with conversations. When he stayed in ashrams where the *sadhus*, yogis and holy men gathered to sing and chant, he found he did not want to emulate those with dreadlocked hair and bodies covered with ash. Though he tried smoking *ganja*, he did not like the effect on his mind, and he saw no value in abusing his body by standing on one foot or holding his arms in the air until his limbs atrophied. When he observed the yogis who lived lives of extreme discipline and bizarre acts of deprivation, the old man knew this was not his path. He also did not enjoy the endless rituals of bowing to statues, burning incense, lighting *puja* fires, and ringing bells, as they seemed a digression from his search for a soul connection with a living teacher. When the old man visited temples run by priests who were not content or kind, he watched them eat and drink to excess and demand offerings from the poor, and he did not want to be part of a religion that served the needs of the priests.

When he tried to communicate what he was looking for to other seekers, he could see they did not understand why he did not join them in their practices. "Is there something the matter with me?" he questioned within. "What am I seeking? How will I find what I am looking for? I only have this sense that when I find it I will know."

As the weeks went by, the old man's pilgrimage became an editing of what he did not want, as well a refining clarity of what he was seeking. He returned to the repetitive logic of a student, and found himself repeating the same phrases, as though he hoped the power of his words would somehow take him to his goal.

"I want a teacher to show me the way. I want to find a teacher who lives and breathes spirituality. I want a true path to prepare me for my passing from this world."

And so the old man walked on, leaving the temples and the priests, the rituals and the discussions behind. He returned to solitude and contemplation, ever exploring his mind and thoughts, ever freeing himself from his previous life, and ever opening into the unknown mystery of his seeking.

At times, a certain place or event enchanted him, as if a vortex of power spun him into the center of a force so potent, he could only sink to the ground and feel the energy of the place: the high-pitched singing of crickets; the fluttering wings of hundreds of small birds flying as one, from treetop to treetop; a storm of golden butterflies landing around him, circling him, alighting on his hands and head; millions of ladybugs creating a red wave on a sandy bank, and an ominous line of vultures on a hill writing a black signature against the sunset sky. Sometimes the eyes of a child or the light around a holy man enraptured him. A sense of tender feeling absorbed these events deep into his being, and he was grateful for the freedom that allowed him the opportunity to witness and be part of each beauty offering.

"To think I had this person inside of me all the years of my life. All that I subdued has broken free and it is as if I have become my opposite, but what pleases me most is that my capacity to love keeps expanding. I am happier than I have ever been but it is not a selfish happiness. I am more aware of others and feel close to them. Oh, how wonderful to shed that busy life that sustained me for so long. Perhaps I will feel the same relief when I shed this body."

When he lay down to sleep each night, he offered his body to the earth, and yet each morning when he awoke, he was glad for one more day. As he listened to the sounds of life around him, drank in the endless flow of sights, and allowed love to flow from him into the essence of life that enveloped him, he felt the pulse of the Creator and his own place in the Creation.

Once, after a day of clay baking, he rubbed himself with mango skins and fell asleep under a tree. On waking in the night, he felt a soft movement on his skin and discovered that he was covered with hundreds of velvety soft, winged moths. He lay still under this living robe, in love with their tender wings, imagining their communal, blind seeking for the warmth still burning in his body. In awe of the beauty and privilege of their restless resting on his skin, he strove to stay awake, yet he fell asleep under their gentle fluttering. When he awoke in the morning, the moths had flown away, but the gentle grace of their visitation remained like a blessing.

As the high summer heat intensified over the parched lands, the old man walked more slowly and rested more often. He discovered opportunity for wonder and awe wherever he found himself because there was always so much to see and hear and feel and know – whether he looked closely at what was around him or far into the mountains or the sky.

"There is nothing I have that I would not give someone if they wanted it," he thought. "Perhaps this is the beginning of surrender," he wondered, as he opened to embrace whatever came before him.

Regardless of where he slept, what shape or size the stones, how hard the earth or floor, how rough the grass or hay, his ability to adjust enabled him to accept and find comfort because of the inner song of his heart. "This is the person I always wanted to be," he murmured as he fell asleep each night. "This is the adventure I have always wanted to live."

Once he caught a glimpse of himself in a mirror as he walked through a market, and he did not recognize himself in the wild, burnished *sadhu* that stared back at him. "I am being dyed in the color of India," he thought, and then he added, "I have come far, but not far enough," and wondered once more when he would find what he was seeking.

It seemed that the vitality of the young, the endurance of the parents and workers, the dignity of the elders, and the suffering of the people had became a part of him. In the villages he witnessed the hard labor of the farmers and their women burdened by carrying fuel and water in their struggle to survive.

In the towns he observed craftsmen and haggling market vendors, desperate for sales. He caught glimpses of shaved widows in white saris living leftover lives, and faces lined with despair peered at him from windows and doorways. No matter how much suffering the villagers endured, their children still ran and played, full of the promise of life and yet imprisoned in the pain and struggle that would one day limit and wound them as all are wounded in the womb of creation.

"So much sorrow. So much hunger. So much struggle," the old man mourned. "Where do the people find the time to know God?"

As the old man journeyed, he witnessed the lives of those in want, the old and infirm, the poor, the sick, and the dying. He heard voices that howled in grief, quarreled in anger, and raved in madness, as well as priests' incantations, babies and children crying and laughing, and the groans of lovemaking that sounded like suffering. And he knew he could have been anyone and anyone could have been him.

In the early days of his pilgrimage, whenever he passed through towns and villages, the odors of exhaust fumes, decaying refuse, and the stench of latrines and sewage had revolted him, so he chose pathways that led through nature into more desolate spaces. After a time, even the raw stench of India was easier to accept, as he opened further to the struggles, suffering, and hardships of the people.

As his connection with nature and the many people of his country expanded, the old man understood even more deeply how the cycles of life nourish each other. "I have become a student of life and death," he pondered, imagining his body as fuel for the flame of the funeral pyre, and how the fluids of his body would steam into the air, and the ashes of his bones and tissues would be gifted to the earth. The scriptures speak of earth-to-earth, water-to-water, fire-to-fire, air-to-air, but there is more to death than that. "What will death feel like? Where will my soul go? How will I meet God?"

The old man sought understanding within himself. "We are born hungry, and like all living creatures, we eat and drink and deposit waste. When we die our bodies return to nature. Millions have gone into death and millions more will continue to be born and die. Why do we know so little of life and death? Why do we pretend we will never die? So few break through to greater longings, and ever fewer to divine union. We lose ourselves in the passions of desire, in the suffering of fear, and in the madness of ignorance, or is it simply forgetfulness? Oh, how I long to get beyond this ignorance of the human condition, and find the way to my divine soul," the old man prayed.

Even though the old man talked to *sadhus*, asked questions of holy men, and listened to the discourses of gurus, nowhere did his heart sing and nowhere did he sigh and say, "Ah hah, this is what I have been seeking." So he continued his journey, heading north toward the Himalayas, thinking, "Perhaps there I will find my path. Perhaps my teacher is in a holy place and I will find him there.

Perhaps today is the day!"

India's rich tapestry of life unraveled before him, but he was walking within it, not separate in an expensive car, not a well-dressed, well-fed, educated landowner and government official, but one of the many. Yet he seemed to be walking between worlds: part and yet not part of it all; visible, yet invisible; known but not known, as though he had already traveled to the land of death. There was only one role left and only one journey: the journey of his soul.

At times when he fell asleep under a tree, someone placed a mango or a banana on his blanket, or if he was sitting and resting by a wall or a well, a passerby dropped a coin. Young mothers shared their *chapatis* when he carried a basket or helped them with their myriad tasks. A laughing child offered a sweet as he rested by a well, and another time an old man invited him to sit for a while in his garden and share tea and pleasant conversation.

During the intense days before the monsoon, when the heat of summer burned without relief, the old man sheltered in a cave. He lay on the earth, his blanket beneath him, watching the sky, shaped by the entrance of the cave, change from a night of bright stars to a day of burning sun and back again. Still, the sky relentlessly refused to offer rain. Those who noticed him left offerings, and a spring provided him with water. He grew thin, but he did not mind as he enjoyed the passive waiting and stillness. He shed his clothes as even they seemed too great a burden in the fire of high summer, and he did not miss the touch of cloth.

When he was not sitting in meditation or sleeping or gazing at the changing sky, he was entertained by the micro-life in the cave. He watched the spiders weaving their webs across the entrance of the cave, observed the erratic buzzing patterns of flies, and delighted in the scattering, fearful mice peeking out from their hiding places then running past him or over him at full speed. Trails of ants seemed fiercely determined and blindly focused, fully participating in the imprisonment of their species. "Perhaps I was like them," he thought as he remembered his days of duty. "It was as though I had blinders on. I thought only of doing my work and fulfilling my duty, and was unaware, like the ants, of everything else around me."

"Noticing the little things," he muttered aloud, "takes time and stillness. And when I notice the small things, I discover they make up the bigger picture, and so they are more important than they seem."

Once again, the old man became lost in contemplation, not minding if the ants traveled over his toes or the flies buzzed around his head or a mouse jumped over his lap. However, even with his new understanding, he became hyper vigilant whenever the spiders approached.

"l am afraid of spiders," he admitted to himself, and so was not surprised when his arm swelled with a bite. "Even spiders feel my fear," the old man thought as he resolved to restore peace to his sheltering cave. Instead of fearing the spiders and shuddering if they came near him, he sent waves of love to the spiders and admired the beauty of their webs, and it must have worked because he did not receive another bite.

"There are dangerous creatures. I see them and know they are there – the scorpions; the centipedes; the snakes; the spiders, and the barking, frothing dogs – and yet I must trust I will be taken care of at the same time as accepting the Lord's will. Such a mystery! Such a paradox! Will I ever understand anything? At least, I have learned to accept all creatures as part of nature and my life journey, and perhaps they have learned to accept me."

One day, after some pilgrims walked slowly past his cave, the old man imagined his son passing by but not recognizing him. "I am no longer myself," he mused. "I am already dying. Every day a little more of me disappears, and every day I prepare to welcome death."

And then the rains came and he danced in the torrents of water, his feet deep in mud, his face open to the force of the water, giving thanks that he could begin his journey once more.

AUTUMN

The monsoon season passed and harvest spread golden upon the land. The nights were cold, as shorter days hurried towards wintering. Rolls of hay lined the shorn fields, and multi-colored leaves scattered with brusque rustles as the old man walked the farmland paths. The air was as crisp as the drying grasses that whispered in the gusts of winds from the northern mountains that made the old man shiver when the sun disappeared behind the clouds. The cawing of birds seemed more strident. Dogs howled at the moon. Mounds of dung patties, spiraled high in the farmyards, promised warmth in farmhouse fires over the coming winter.

Through the day, the old man wore his long cotton underwear and his sweater, and in the morning he clutched his shawl and blanket around him until the sun's warmth rose in the sky toward noon. As cold left its imprint on the land, the old man accepted the baring of branches as the fluttering of leaves and winged seeds followed the wind over the overturned earth in the emptying fields. Although he felt the signs of approaching winter heralded the death he must soon face, he did not contract in fear. Instead, he felt an inner opening and a love that was bountiful.

"I am coming to love endings," the old man realized as he felt a longing for his own spiritual harvest. "When my time comes, my body that was gathered into form by the elements of life will release: my earth will become part of this earth; my warmth will dissipate; my air will become one with the sky; my fluids will flow with the waters; my body will become a part of everything. That is why I know my soul will also want to fly home."

As he had these thoughts and said these words, he felt an internal shift. A knot of fear he had not known he had carried all his life unraveled and flew free. The old man felt his heart open in trust, and he inhaled a great breathing in and sighed a great breathing out as if at last his breath had united in one full circle. "Death happens little by little," he discovered, and he offered gratitude for the grace to be present with the changes happening within him.

The generous harvest glowed upon the land and in the eyes and hearts of the farmers and villagers. Celebration was in the air. The harshness of daily toil was temporarily eclipsed by their shared pride as workers gathered grain and produce, filling heavily laden trucks that the farmers drove to market. The men were spare and lean, hardened by their intense struggles against capricious weather, water shortages and excesses, landowners' greed, government officials' bribes, and fluctuating prices that overshadowed their daily fears of crop failure, poverty, starvation, accidents, and illness. Even so, their faces shone with courage in the autumn glow as they harvested the fruits of their labor. The hope in their eyes was fed by the pride for their women as they walked towards them in the fields, swaying, holding jars of water on their head with one hand while they carried a *tiffin* filled with lunch in the other. Moments like this were the glory of their lives and the sustenance that supported the birthing, raising, marrying, and dying within the walls of their family compounds.

The old man offered assistance to the farmers. He joined in the harvest whenever he passed a farm, and at lunch he sat on the ground and listened to their discussions while the women sat shyly at a distance. In the evenings he slept in the fields or sheltered in a barn. Pleasantly tired from the work, his heart full of the courage and resilience of the people, he contemplated his own harvest and the reaping of his soul.

"Just like the chaff, my body will fall to the ground, but where will my soul go? Everything in life teaches me something about spirituality. Everywhere I go, I see reflections of my seeking and find the meaning of my journey, but I still don't understand how to prepare for death. You would think after thousands of generations, humanity would understand the life of the soul. We pray for everything in life, but how many of us pray to find our soul? Religion keeps us from the truth, work steals our time, and our family takes the rest of our attention. Where will I find the truth? How will I find the way to my soul?"

And finally, weary with questions he could not answer, the old man fell asleep, thinking, "Perhaps tomorrow will be the day. Perhaps I will find my teacher tomorrow."

In the morning when the old man woke in a grove of trees, a teenage boy was sitting before him, watching him, apparently waiting for him to wake up.

"*Namasté*, young man," the old man said, "Where have you come from?"

"I ran away from home two days ago, but now I don't know where to go."

"Why did you run away?"

"I don't want to work in the fields and marry and have children and die. I want to live a spiritual life. I want to find a teacher, live in a temple, study scriptures, pray and be a holy man of God," the young man exclaimed in one breath.

The old man was stunned for a moment, and he looked at the young man carefully. He had an open, clear face and sincere, passionate eyes. He looked scared, but the old man could sense the boy's courage and determination. For a moment the old man had the odd feeling that he was looking at himself in his youth if he had not been too afraid to go against his father's will.

"And what do your parents think about this?"

"My father demanded that I work in the fields but I have four brothers. They don't need me, but, they don't want to let me go, and so I ran away."

"Where are you headed? Have you been to any temples? Have you asked any priests for sanctuary?"

"No, I wanted to walk far from my village so that my family couldn't find me. My parents believe we must stay together as a family, and work together and die together, but I feel another call. I want to serve God and help others. I want a simple life and time to read the holy books and devote myself to prayer."

"I did too, dear boy, but I didn't pay attention to it when I was your age. I was bound by duty and was also afraid to leave my family. I didn't feel the call until this spring, and now I am an old man seeking his death, using the time I have left to look for my path and my teacher too, just like you."

"I thought you were a *sadhu*, a devotee of God. I saw you sleeping so peacefully on the ground under the tree, and I knew you were a good person. Will you let me come with you?"

"Yes, you are welcome to join me. The winter is coming and we have to find shelter. Perhaps together we will find what we are looking for," the old man said as he got up and folded his blanket. "You are very brave to go against your parents' wishes."

"I may look like I am brave, but I didn't have a choice. I have to find a place where I can live a spiritual life."

"Yes, I know that feeling. When the call comes, we have to seek what our heart and soul are yearning for. Come along, young man," the old man said, as he gathered his things. "Let's see what the road brings today. And if I am going to travel with you, what is your good name?"

"They call me Hari. And yours?"

Just call me Chacha, dear boy. Just think of me as your uncle."

And so the old man and the young man set off down the road. They talked for a while, and then fell into a comfortable silence as they walked through farmlands and villages; past streams; over roads and along paths, walking strongly, but noticing all that came before them.

For the first time on his pilgrimage, the old man was the more experienced guide. He enjoyed sharing stories of his adventures on the road and showing Hari how to gather roots and make soups over their evening fire, all the while delighting in the bright open face and pure heart of the young man. Hari's story of leaving his family touched his heart because he understood the chains of family attachment and the duties that hold you back from exploring your own longings for another way of life.

"I hid my longings," the old man said, "but even though you were open in asking your family for education and the chance to devote yourself to the spiritual life, in the end you had to leave without their permission."

"Yes, and it goes against our traditions as

you know. Family is so important because it is how we survive, but I do not want to live in fear of crop failure, starvation and government controls. I don't want to marry the girl they chose for me and bear the burdens of wife and children. The friends I grew up with can think of nothing else than the day of their marriage, but the closer I came to that day the more urgently I needed to depart. Just like you, I woke up one morning and knew I had to leave."

"We are being called by something greater than reason or duty," the old man reassured his young companion. "It seems we are two of a kind, and we must follow the path that is opening before us. Did you feel close to anyone in your family?"

"I adored my sister. She is full of life and intelligence. I will miss her, but I am glad I do not have to watch her spirit diminish. My parents arranged her marriage to an older, wealthy man, but he was not a good man. She did not have a choice. She had to accept the destiny my father arranged for her. I believe my mother understood me and would have liked to support me in my choice. Her eyes glowed with love and understanding when she looked at me, but she never said a word against my father's wishes. Her path is submission and I respect that. My path is to strike out and find the life that is calling me," the young man exclaimed with passion. "Perhaps I am the part of her that would have loved to adventure into new worlds. I like to think she is secretly happy that I escaped."

"I wonder why we have to make such choices,"

the old man answered. "I would have loved to live a life that merged spirituality into daily life, but I never felt any connection to my soul with my family's Hindu rituals. I want to find a path and a teacher that stir my heart and show me truth. I want to know how to find my soul before I die."

And so, conversations and questions punctuated their easy silence, as though the young man and the old man continued their discussions within until the depth of their iceberg thoughts required surfacing and sharing with each other.

One evening as they sat before a fire in a sheltered canyon, the old man asked Hari, "How did it begin, this longing, and this separation of ways from your family life?"

"It was always that way. I was the youngest and I grew up hearing them complain when they returned exhausted after a day's labor. I listened to all the stories of hardship and struggle and saw that they never got ahead. They worked so hard and had so little time to enjoy life and family, and they were never kind to their women. Even my father expected too much from my mother when she was ill. It was a harsh life. I never wanted to work in the fields from dawn to dusk, but my brothers never questioned their destiny. As long as they had their meals, their *bidi* cigarettes, their beer, and their women, they accepted their life, even though they got angry about the prices they were paid for their produce and grains. They hated the government officials and raged at the politics that controlled their lives, but they couldn't change anything. I don't want to live in anger. It was no life for me."

"You had a separate destiny and yet you were meant to be raised in a farm."

"Yes, I never regretted that, especially as the youngest in a joint family. There was always someone to cuddle me, carry me, and give me treats."

"You were very fortunate," commented the old man.

"Yes, I was, but even from the beginning, I could see the life they lived was not the life for me. Because I was the baby, they spoiled me and tolerated my games, my singing, and my jokes. I liked to make them laugh when they came in tired and hungry after their long hours in the fields, but I also learned how to get what I wanted with my charms. I convinced my father to send me to school so that I could do the bookkeeping and write letters. When he found I had no fear of the landowners, he sent me on errands of negotiation. But when they took me out of school to work in the fields, I had to leave. I have no regret and will never return. Some may find that strange but I know the life I must live. It has always been that way."

As the days passed, the winds from the north harried the travelers, and they bent their heads down as they pressed against its force. Leaves swirled around them as trees revealed their branching structure against a dimmer sky. Green faded into browns as fields empty of harvest shaded toward earth. Pale grey clouds dominated the skies as the sun retreated its warmth. However, their companionship warmed their hearts and encouraged their faith as they walked briskly, shawls wrapped tightly around them as they shared their dreams and hopes for a spiritual life.

When they spent the night in the fields, they built fires and took turns keeping the flames alive throughout the night. They exchanged labor for shelter whenever they could, but they knew they could not continue much longer on the road. Sometimes they joined other wanderers, *sadhus* and seekers and sought shelter in temples where the passage of night was filled with the sounds of breathing, coughing, and sighing. In the mornings when the travelers gathered around *chai* and hot cereal, they shared stories of the road and possible places for their wintering; yet when the day warmed, the old man delighted in his wandering seeking with the young man, and postponed the shadow of change looming under the lowering autumn sun.

And then one day, as the afternoon warmth receded before the advancing dusk, they came to an open plain where a path led up a hill to a small temple. The old man turned to the young man and said, "I think we are supposed to go there."

The young man turned to the old man and said, "I think so too."

As they walked up the incline, the sunset tinted the dome of the temple with a golden rosy glow. An elderly priest dressed in saffron robes walked out and bowed before them.

"I have been expecting you. Come in. You are most welcome."

They entered the carved temple door into a room circled by arched windows. At the back, a rectangular room harbored an open stove in a small kitchen, and sleeping benches. After the old man and the young boy washed and refreshed themselves, they sat before the fire and the meal made ready for them.

The priest served *dal* and *chapatis* and poured hot milk into their cups. They ate slowly, absorbing the gentle atmosphere, and the beauty of the last rays of the sun glowing through the arched windows into the circular room.

The priest turned to the young man and said, "So, you have come to me?"

The young man answered, "Yes, may I stay here with you?"

The priest smiled, "Yes, it is your home now. It is time to prepare to leave this sanctuary in good hands. This temple has always welcomed pilgrims and travelers. Taking care of the temple and gardens is our main work, and there is plenty of time for meditation and the study of the scriptures. The life here is a good and holy life."

The young man bowed his head and brought his arms together at his heart in thanks, and the old man could see he was trembling with emotion.

As dark settled around them, a holy peace

filled the room. The young man lay down before the fire and was soon asleep. The priest and the old man sat in a silence infused with wonder at the purity of the young man's heart.

"Will you stay with us?" the priest asked the old man, after a time.

"No, thank you. I too must find my place. I will set out in the morning." The old man offered his excuses abruptly as he felt embarrassed to refuse the kind offer. The priest smiled, but his penetrating glance made the old man shiver.

"What are you looking for?" the priest questioned, with another piercing look that sent shock waves through the old man's body.

"My spiritual home, a true path, a true teacher, to guide me toward my death," the old man whispered without looking at the monk.

"Then, yes, you must continue on your journey. I will give you my blessing." The priest rose and placed his hands on the old man's head, whispering mantras that echoed through the temple.

The old man received the priest's blessing with gratitude, but felt an immediate aching hunger, as if the longing for his spiritual home was now tainted by a fear that he might not find it. He lay upon the mat provided for him and covered himself with his shawl and blanket. As tears welled in his eyes he thought, "I am like a young boy myself. I feel like a child. I don't understand the mystery of life and death. I don't know where I'm going or if I will find what I am looking for." The thought that he might never find his teacher surged within him, and the feeling was so unbearable that he could not sleep.

The boy next to him breathed softly and evenly like a child who knows he is safe. The old man had witnessed the boy's good fortune in finding his teacher, and he thought it would give him hope; yet there was a sense of unease within the old man, as though a viper stirred within him. When he closed his eyes, disjointed images of his life passed before him, but whenever he opened his eyes, he saw the priest sitting in meditation, first like a shadow in the dark and then illuminated under the light of the winter moon.

"Oh, if only I could be still, at rest in body and in mind. Maybe I should stay here, take refuge for the winter, and learn from this priest," he considered for a moment, but that thought only made him more restless because it activated questions and fears. The old man struggled to keep still and quiet when all he wanted to do was toss and turn and moan in a floodtide of despair.

When dawn glowed golden through the arched temple windows, the old man did not ask to stay. He rose quietly, gathered his things, and bid the priest and the young boy a hurried goodbye. He fled the beautiful temple and fine company so they would not discover his confused agitation and tempt him to stay.

WINTER

As he walked quickly down the hill onto the plain, the old man argued with himself. "Perhaps I don't need to fear the winter or worry that I will not find my teacher. I witnessed my young friend find his spiritual home. This should inspire me and help me to trust that I too will reach my goal."

But then, a little later he felt the opposite, "But I have been walking for months and still I have not reached my goal. It is so cold at night. What will I do?"

The old man missed his young companion. "I always enjoyed being alone before, even sought it, but now I feel lonely. Where is the enthusiasm that has carried me thus far? Why could we not have found a place where we could have stayed together?" he mourned, allowing desolation to overtake him.

Further down the road, he returned to trust. "I must remember I have been taken care of so many times. I have been protected, sheltered, and welcomed during my journey. I felt the presence of grace surround me when I was in danger. I must believe I am being led to my heart's desire."

The old man received some comfort from his reasoning, but underneath the viper stirred, and the fear that he would not find his teacher raced through his mind once more. Soon panic overtook him, and he perspired even though he was cold. For the first time in many long months, he was not enjoying his pilgrimage. He felt only discomfort, anxiety, agitation and restlessness.

"I will not allow this fear to take over my mind," he whispered intensely, as he drew his shawl and blanket closely around him and gathered his will. He sought to recover the blend of passionate trust, faith, and enchantment that had carried him through his journey to this day, but the circling raven thoughts had a power that resisted all attempts to tame them.

As the old man strode north in the bitter cold morning, his will drew on the well of his heart to melt his agitated mind, and a flood of soft, sweet thoughts and memories mingled with the power of his longing and gave him strength. The longing enlivened his purpose and helped him struggle against his doubts. Eventually, the surge of will gained dominance and carried him through the day, but he could not sleep that night as he wavered between the excited anticipation that he might find his spiritual home and the fear that he might not. Torn by conflict between two potent opposites, the old man could not wait for the dawn. He set off from the bus shelter where he had huddled during the night into the sharp, cold morning wind. Unlike the slow pace of his wandering summer, he strode with a nervous speed that matched the tumult in his mind, as if he thought he could outrun his anguish.

In his unbalanced state, every time he remembered that the young man had found shelter with his teacher, the memory took on the quality of a vision from the gods that meant he too would reach his goal. He felt as though he might find it at any moment, and an agitated excitement overwhelmed him only to be followed by immediate despair.

"Perhaps today is the day," the old man thought, and then he worried, "but what if I already passed it, just missing it?" He turned around and spun in a circle, questioning his path. "But no, just like the priest called the young man to him, perhaps my teacher is calling me and guiding me and waiting for me. I must trust. I must believe."

This thought spun the old man's mind into a euphoria that set his mind afire with expectation and questions. "What will my teacher be like? Where will my spiritual home be? Will I be able to stay there through the cold of the winter?"

But then the fears returned. "What if the Master is not there? What if he goes south for the winter? What if they close the ashram in the cold weather? What if they are full and have no room for me to stay?"

Through the day, the anxiety increased, until the old man was in an agony of doubt. His body could not bear the burning conflict, and he felt weak and dizzy.

"My mind is wild, uncontrollable, and I

can do nothing about it," he raged, adding anger, frustration, and impatience into the field of conflict that had overtaken him.

The second night was so cold that his breath blew misting clouds into the darkness. The burden of fear and anger had unbalanced him. He had given no thought to food since he had left the priest's temple. Exhausted but tense like a coiled spring, he could not bear the agony, but did not know how to stop it, and he could not sleep. The cold increased, but the burning in his body and his brain did not keep him warm. Both the cold and the heat felt like needles, and the fever increased the freezing shivering. He had not given a thought for shelter that night, so he huddled against a wall, shaking, rubbing his body, overcome by the suffering of burning and cold that mirrored his hungry longing and his fear.

Then a thought flew across his mind like the shadow of a vulture in the sky. "I must be going mad." This new fear increased the darkness in his mind and made the viper within him stir with a strength that terrified him.

"What is this madness in my brain? Is it only fear? No, it is rage and impatience. It is doubt and grief, and it is all darkness. And the worst feeling is my helplessness. I don't know what's real, or if any of it is real? Holy men say everything in this world is illusion. This must be true, because I do not know who I am, where I am, why I am doing what I am doing. It was childish to think an old man like me could find a teacher and a true path. Why am I am out here in this freezing weather when I could be in my comfortable family home? Just think of their happiness if I returned. My son and my grandchildren would be overjoyed. My room is warm, and there is food, and servants to take care of me. There is no reason to continue this journey. I am going home. If I took a bus or a train, I could be home tomorrow."

As the sun sent its first rays into the brightening sky, the old man shook with the cold and the fever that burned within him. He looked for a moment at the distant foothills of the Himalayas as though to bid farewell to a dream that no longer held him in its power, and he turned south toward his ancestral home.

"I will never find the teacher I dream of," he decided. "It is time I woke up and stopped being a child in this old body. It is time to go home and let my family take care of me." A sob caught in his throat, and tears stung his eyes. "I don't have much time left. It is time to go home and die."

The old man strode south toward the low, wintering sun, but giving up and returning home did not ease his mind because his doubts and questions only increased. "What if I were only a mile away, right now? What if I turned back and never knew how close I was? But I am weak and ill, and this journey has gone on too long. It is too cold. I must find shelter. I need to go home."

And so the old man continued south, his neck wrapped in a woolen scarf and his feet enclosed in two pairs of woolen socks. Even with both sets of his pants and *kurtas* worn over his long cotton underwear, and his pullover, shawl and blanket drawn close around him, he shivered in the harsh winds and bitterly cold air. The icy drafts from the mountains blew strong all morning, as if pushing him south, and the cold increased when the sun disappeared behind dark clouds.

By noon, the old man felt weak. He had not eaten in two days, and his tongue was dry with thirst. He had not met any pilgrims on the road this morning, only scurrying villagers seeking shelter. They had not given him a glance or offered him even so much as a *chapati*, or a seat before their fires, and he was too distressed to ask, and so he pressed on determined to reach a town where he could find a train or a bus and cease his endless wandering.

His body ached with fever, exhaustion, and hunger and although the burden of conflict weighed on him, the fearful questioning lessened as every part of him focused on walking, on putting one foot before the other. This day, he did not notice nature, children, the farmhands, or villagers. He did not admire the weather or scan the sky for cloud patterns or the flights of birds. No philosophies or enchantments lightened his heart. He had shut himself within his will and trimmed himself away from connection. There was only one vision now, a home that offered shelter, food, and warmth.

By mid afternoon the old man felt faint and looked around. "I must find food. I must find a place to rest, away from this wind and this cold."

As he came around a corner in the road, he

saw a small, well-kept farmhouse with smoke rising like a plume into the dull, winter sky, its gardens enclosed by a low wall. Spirals of dung patties promised a warm fire; and the cow in the yard meant milk, cheese, and yoghurt. The thought of a chapati fresh from the oven in his cold hands made him swoon, and he staggered as he neared the gate. He glimpsed a woman standing in the open doorway, and then he fell.

He heard women's voices as he was being lifted and carried inside the farmhouse. Then he felt a soft mat under him and blankets covering him. Kind hands rubbed his feet then placed hot stones wrapped in cloth near them. The soft warmth enclosed him as gentle hands lifted his head. A few sips of tea, and then a tunnel opened and he fell into darkness.

Soft murmuring voices, quiet footsteps, and the crackling of a fire hovered near the old man's consciousness as if in a dream. The relief of softness, warmth and rest made him feel like he floated on a cloud in a dream. He tried to turn over, but his body would not respond and he fell into the tunnel again.

The old man felt the sensation of warm light pouring over him. He struggled to open his eyes, but the light was too bright, and he lifted his arm to shield his eyes. More whispering voices, the laugh of a child, water splashing: all sensations calling him to awaken, but the fatigue held him heavy in gravity, and he had no power to return.

A hand on his forehead, the warm comfort of a

moist cloth on his face, the scent of a woman and the rustle of her sari before she held a cup of broth to his lips penetrated the fog that surrounded him, but still he could not rise to consciousness. His awareness lingered near the surface but would not awaken.

A first thought formed, "I am still here. I can continue my pilgrimage." Then he fell into the darkness again. Later, the quiet stillness of night comforted him, and then the morning light shone again.

A child's voice penetrated the deep, healing sleep of the old man, and he felt himself slowly awakening to her song. He opened his eyes and saw a young girl, perhaps two or three years old, sitting near him, singing and clapping her hands. She jumped up when she saw his eyes open and laughed.

"We thought you would never wake up, but my song worked. Mama! Amma!" the little girl called, "He is awake. See, my song woke him up," and she danced about the room. A young woman peered in the door, shyly pulling her shawl around her face. She smiled, but did not say anything.

Then an older woman came into the room. She was perhaps his own age, or younger, with a serene, kind face. Her white hair waved smoothly back from an untroubled brow, and she wore a violet sari with a silver border, and a matching violet woolen cardigan. He took in every detail in a glance: her grace, the colors of violet and silver, and the sheen of a loving, caring radiance.

"Welcome," she said softly with a gentle smile,

her right hand reaching up to adjust her sari as she moved closer. "My name is Indra. Don't speak. We will talk later. First, you must eat, drink and gather strength. You have been sleeping for two days." She reached out and touched his forehead, "Yes, the fever is down. This is very good."

"Jyoti, bring the soup, my dear," she called affectionately, and the young mother entered the room, sat beside him, and began to spoon warm broth into his mouth.

Intervals of sleeping, waking, eating, drinking, and sleeping again cycled for another day and night. Each time the old man awoke, he felt more alert, and slowly his strength returned. Sometimes he sat up and watched the family, enjoying the harmony of the women as they moved about their tasks. The little girl, Chandra, often sat with him – talking, singing, and keeping him company – and he felt nourished by the bright joy of her happiness.

Once when the grandmother came near, the old man looked at her and asked gently, "Where are your men?"

"I am a widow. My husband died a few years ago, and Jyoti's husband is in the army, so we don't see him often, but we enjoy our simple life here and are grateful for what we have." She smiled such a sweet smile that it reached deeply into his heart and awakened the tenderness he had missed since his wife passed.

"You manage all alone, even with the animals and gardens?"

"Yes, we enjoy the work, and sometimes we

hire boys from the other farms, but we prefer to keep to ourselves whenever we can. And of course, we have family nearby, but more often than not, they are just trouble. We enjoy a simple life and we are happiest on our own." Indra gestured to their altar, "And you see, we have our Krishna to bless our lives."

"Yes, you have all you need here. Thank you for taking me in," he offered, as tears welled in his eyes.

"You fell at our door, and so it was our destiny to take care of you," she replied with a smile, her eyes sparkling as she rose in one graceful movement. "Where were you going?"

"I have been on a spiritual pilgrimage since April. I have been looking for a teacher and a path to lead me through my passing from this world. The day I came here was the day I had turned back to return to my ancestral home."

"You gave up?"

"Yes. Something happened after I stayed for a night in a temple not too many miles from here. The priest gave me a blessing, but after I left, I was filled with fear and doubt. I had been enjoying my adventure and all that the road offered to me, and after that one night, my joy vanished. Conflict tore me apart until I was burning with fever in my body and my mind. I was taken over by wild thoughts, fears and questions. It was agony. I could not bear it. I could not eat. I could not sleep. I burned and I froze. I shivered and grew weak, and you know the rest. I fell at your door."

"Do you understand what happened?"

"No, not really. I felt like I had a viper inside me, like poison was spreading through me. I could not control my mind, but I cannot say I understand it."

"Then think about it. You traveled for months without doubt, it seems, convinced you would seek and find what you were looking for. The priest showed you the other side of the picture," she said with a laugh that rang through the farmhouse. "Perhaps it was a test," she laughed again. "How do you feel now? Do you still have doubts?"

"No, my mind seems to be at peace."

"That is very good, and when you are strong, you can decide which way to go," Indra said as she turned to leave. Then she hesitated and looked at the old man as she added, "And then, perhaps it was all part of the divine plan that you found your way here, to our home." And then she slipped away leaving him to wonder what she meant.

The old man rested for a while, exploring and enjoying the sensation of emptiness. He waited for a feeling that would tell him whether to keep seeking or return to his family, but nothing came to him so he dozed off again. When he awoke, he lifted himself carefully to his feet and took a few steps. He walked to the door and looked out. The sun shone warmly. The two women were working in the garden while Chandra played with their dog. Then Chandra saw him and called out to her mother and grandmother, and the women came to him and took his arms and walked him through the garden.

"You see it is warmer now," Indra said. "You

have a few more days to seek your teacher, and perhaps you will find him. Often we find what we are looking for when we are ready to give up. We have heard of a great teacher not far from here. Many seekers pass by. Why don't you head that way and see what you find?" Indra said, pointing toward the foothills of the Himalayas a little to the east. "You see that road, there! That is the one the pilgrims take to the Holy City. It is perhaps a two or three days walk, depending on how fast you go. I am sure you will meet other pilgrims who will be glad to guide you on your way."

This news stirred the old man's heart and he felt a leap of hope. The old man enjoyed the company of the three generations of women as he gained strength, and two days later. he was ready to leave. The good weather encouraged him to take the road Indra indicated, and he felt the thrill of possibility surge through him. He placed his last rupees under the sleeping mat as an offering of gratitude, and bowed deeply as he said his farewells.

With her hands together at her heart, Indra said, "I wish you many blessings for your pilgrimage."

Jyoti, whispered, "*Namasté*," as she looked shyly at the ground, her shawl nearly obscuring her face. Chandra danced a few steps down the lane with the old man and then let go of his hand. She continued to sing and wave and the old man waved back at her until she passed from view at the turn in the road.

And so, the old man's journey continued, and although it was the same journey, he felt different. The enchantment seemed less, and then he realized he had always been full of excitement, and anticipation, like a child. Now, he was calmer. "I see now that I was more in love with my own adventure, than with my seeking. Ah, so many lessons to learn, even now," the old man thought with a pang of sorrowful humility. "Perhaps that is why I did not find my teacher before."

"Even as I am old and dying, I am a child who needs instruction," he thought. "Even though everyone I meet is my teacher and I am always learning from nature, I still feel I must find a spiritual teacher to guide me toward my last days." These words awoke a vision of the cells of his body being scattered into creation at his death, and his soul rising like a fragrance. "This is what I see in my mind, and this is what I am searching for."

"I was taken care of in a time of great need by Indra and her family, and I am being taken care of now," he thought, as tears of happiness gathered in his eyes. "Love is everywhere, not just in your own family."

"I could be anyone's father, uncle, grandfather or brother," he thought with compassion. Greeting fellow travelers with kindness, sharing what he had and helping out whenever he could, had increased the love he felt growing inside of him. This compassion helped the old man to accept the idea of his death.

"There is a greater love waiting for me – the love of the soul in everyone. I am beginning to understand the love that shines from the holy men and women, the spiritual teachers and the gurus. Their love shines from the source of love, the soul, and it shines equally on everyone."

The next day, he remembered he had given his last rupees away and laughed. "I can't take a bus or a train, so I guess I will have to find shelter with my teacher," he thought, and the humor lightened his heart. "Perhaps today is the day!"

His sense of adventure returned, and he found himself deep in a reverie as he walked. "We are helpless before our birth and helpless before our death, and now I know I was helpless before my destiny that unraveled so quickly," he thought. "Day after day I was swept along never knowing what would happen. Now I know this helplessness is all we have. I have always been in the hands of the divine, only now I give myself fully to this helplessness."

The old man had been raised in a family of love, educated with tutors, graduated from university, traveled the world, been successful in law, engineering, and business, and awarded important posts in government. During his pilgrimage he had disappeared into a dusty, spare *sadhu*, a seeker with no home, no money, no name, no caste. Nobody.

THE HOLY CITY

The old man was startled from the memories of his pilgrimage by a murmur that rose on a crescendo into one pure voice singing a song of longing, a *bhajan*. The poetry of the saints soaring around him in the domed temple, the old man sighed because he realized he had reached the Holy City of his dreams. He had glimpsed the spiritual Master he longed to find, and received his *darshan*. He had found the true path he had been seeking.

As the old man gazed around him, he saw that the temple was fashioned of bricks made from the red earth of the lands around the Holy City. He glanced upward and admired the stained glass that cast a golden glow over the interior. The high ceilings opened into arches where open windows welcomed fresh breezes. A small bird captured in the interior fluttered from window to window, and the old man's heart beat with excitement. Then, as another wave of sound gathered into a single cry of longing, the Master appeared and sat on a low dais, His noble love-truth shining like pure light into the old man's heart. Instantly, the throng settled into silence, as all faces, all eyes, turned to the One who sat before them.

With his gaze offered to the Master, the old man barely saw how the ushers pulled the men up, one by one, for their moment before the Master. Then he felt the usher's arms on his shoulders, and they led him like a child before the Master. The old man trembled, hands pressed together before his heart, held by His eyes.

"You are vegetarian?" the Master asked.

"Yes, Sire."

"You wish initiation?"

"Yes, Sire."

For a moment the Master looked deeply into the old man's eyes, creating a pause that seemed to swirl in a deep knowing of all that he had ever been and would be.

"And where do you live?"

"Nowhere, Sire," he replied, as tears tumbled from a grief so deep his body shook. Yet he held to the Master's eyes and weathered the storm for what seemed an eternity, and then he heard the Master say, "Take him to the management after the initiation." The Master waved his hand, and the ushers led the old man by the arms, one on each side, to a group where another sevadar gave the instructions for the meditation practice. After some time, the Master appeared and chanted the mantra with the new initiates before he bowed, hands to his heart, and left the temple.

His travel-worn sandals, and his dusty blanket

and shawl bundle were returned to him. Then the old man was led in a line of men to the *langar* kitchens for *chai, dal,* and *chapatis*. His body felt light, like he had entered into a stream that was carrying him along in a surge of grace. Everywhere he looked, eyes of happiness shone back at him. Workers attended to tasks with energetic enthusiasm. The streets were spotless. Was he in India? Or was he in a dream?

The old man followed with trust. A bright, young man with laughing eyes guided him to the *Seva* office where a stern, bearded and turbaned Sikh gentleman gave him sheets, a pillow, blanket, and two sets of cotton *kurtas* and pants, marking everything carefully in a huge, leather-bound ledger. Then the young man led him to a building where rooms opened off a bricked courtyard. After opening the door to a room on the ground floor, he bid farewell to the old man. After arranging his belongings and making his bed, the old man lay down. Trembling, he fell inward into waves of radiance that glowed with images of the Master's face.

When the three o'clock siren rang, the old man sat up to practice the morning meditation. Later, after showering, and dressing in his new clothes, he followed the crowds to *satsang*, a blessed hour sitting before the Master. There in that holy gathering, he listened to the Master discourse on the *shabd* sung by the *pathi*. Simple as the teachings were, they were the teachings he had been searching for.

Although the old man focused on receiving the *darshan* glance of the saint that illuminated his soul connection, the words of the *satsang* also penetrated his consciousness. Often a particular phrase, like "... die daily," stayed with him and seamlessly became a part of him.

Although the old man felt the pull of death, he also felt more alive, as though death had become his adventure. "All through my journey, I felt myself dying," the old man remembered. "Now that I have found my path and my teacher, I am ready to die to this world. The Master says that I can do the meditation practice and open the path to my soul so that when my time comes I will know the way." He marveled, "Because of this truth, I no longer fear death. I am ready to open to the light of my soul."

SEASONS OF SERVICE

THE BRICKYARDS

After *satsang* followed by a breakfast of *dal, chapati* and *chai* in the *langar*, the old man was guided to offer his service in the brickyard. There, he set to work breaking bricks, one end of his turban wrapped around his face to protect him from the dust. The days soon followed a regular rhythm. The head *sevadars* guided him, taught him, and told him what to do. Each night, he showered and changed into a clean *kurta* and pants. He threw away the ragged clothes he had worn on his journey, and although his sandals were frayed after months on the road, he was glad of them, as he was of his socks, underwear, sweater, and shawl.

Now that he was sheltered during the night and well dressed in the mornings, he enjoyed the crisp winter weather. The sun often shone through the mists by midday, and the gentle warmth was welcome. Although he huddled around the fires like the other men when it was cold and damp, he found his best remedy in physical activity. He enjoyed the exercise, the work, and the companionship. He walked vigorously along the bricked streets swept clean by aged widows wearing white, cotton saris, to morning *darshan* and *satsang* with the Master, and then to the *langar* for *chai* and breakfast before he rode to the brickyards in the back of a truck with the other *sevadars*. The work energized him and gave purpose to his days. He slept well at night and applied himself to his spiritual practice, and he was always alert for glimpses of the Master.

Winter deepened toward the darkest day of the year, but the old man hardly noticed. He remembered the light in his Master's eyes, and his heart was full even though dust irritated his eyes, his hands became raw from handling the wet mortar and the bricks, and he shivered when it rained. After a time, discomforts lessened as changes in weather began to pass without preference.

He learned to mix and pour clay into molds and break the new bricks free when they had cooled from the heat of the ovens. At other times, the old man sat under spare, leafless trees, grateful for the warmth of the pale winter sun. The red dust sifted over him as he hammered old and broken bricks into rubble, and his hands, once so soft, became calloused. His nails, once manicured, were chipped and broken. No longer the visionary engineer holding rolls of plans, the old man had become an anonymous worker of raw materials who helped make plans come to life.

Each morning, he attended the discourses of the Master, when he was in residence, or with the community when he was not. He listened carefully to the teachings, absorbing their truth, practiced meditation morning and night, and repeated the mantra inwardly during the day. The *darshan* of the Master illuminated the promise of the light of the soul, and the truth of the teachings entwined in his heart and mind. Certain phrases rang like songs within him, to be replaced by others, fresh and new, until they too become a part of him.

"Make good use of this life." The Master's voice rang out strongly as if for his ears alone.

On yet another day, the old man heard the Master say, "The mind is a rogue elephant," and he knew that to be true.

"The purpose of life is God realization," arrived in his heart one morning like an arrow true to its mark from the Master's teaching.

And when the old man heard the Master say, "This is not a path of information. It is a path of transformation," he knew any progress would be the result of meditation. In fact the word he heard most of all was, "Meditation. Meditation. Meditation."

The old man contemplated the teachings of the *satsangs* and thought, "This is a different path than the Master and disciple relationships of the past. It is not a path of dialogue and conversation. It is a path of action, of effort, and of practice. It is up to the disciple to do the work of meditation to still the mind and open to receive the grace of spirituality."

On another day, a phrase made a home in his heart when the Master said, "Even our families become our enemies when we let them keep us from our spiritual practice." The old man nodded with sorrow at the entanglements of human love and how he had let his family keep him from exploring the journey of his soul.

"True as that is," the old man thought, "my time for shedding attachments arrived after my wife's death, painful as it was, because I knew I would soon have to face my own death. Perhaps if I had found this path earlier, I could have found a way to practice a spiritual path and loving detachment within family life."

Sometimes, the old man worried because he had come to the spiritual path so late in life. "I have not had time to still my mind. I have not made enough effort with meditation," but the *satsangs*, the daily meditation, and his service in the brickyards kept him busy, and he let his worries go and trusted his destiny to the Master's teaching and the meditation practice that had been given to him at initiation.

The *satsangs* inspired the old man and he devoted all his spare time to the meditation practice. This focus increased his receptivity to the light he saw emanating from the Master like showers of radiant grace. He absorbed the love that shone from the Master, and that love was mixed into the mortar that the old man placed in the molds that burned into bricks in the ovens and became a part of the Holy City.

From time to time, although he wondered about his ancestral home, his son and his grandchildren, he was not troubled. He could not tell whether his grief for his wife had faded or whether it had dissolved into the light that seemed to be illuminating his inner world. He became aware of a spacious detachment that opened before the compassion that was growing within him, compassion, not only for others, but also for himself.

As the old man mastered the work in the brickyards, he began to feel a part of the cycle of the bricks. Just like the bricks, he too was shaped and formed of earth, and just like the bricks, he too would return to dust. His hands, rough from the touch of earth, shaped bricks from mortar, felt the heat of their burning before the ovens, broke them free of their molds when they cooled, stacked them ready for delivery, and broke the ones destined to return to dust.

The old man rose early in the cold mornings striving to concentrate, to surrender to the practice of meditation, and the repetition of the words. As concentration deepened in his practice, he placed the words in his mind as though they were bricks, one after another, in front of the Master within.

Then one morning after his meditation practice, the old man realized that his work with bricks mirrored the Master's teachings. Just as bricks become walls and buildings to protect inhabitants, the initiation vows protected the disciples. A vegetarian diet, with no alcohol or recreational drugs, combined with moral living were the vows that provided the structure that supported his meditation practice and his service in the spiritual colony.

"What wealth to receive so much before the work day begins," he thought, his heart rejoicing with the fullness of his Master's gifts.

"I have always enjoyed knowing what I must do," he thought. "It keeps life simple, and it is even better to be told what to do," he decided, remembering how his wife loved to manage his life. She always knew what he needed before he did, and he had surrendered to her as he did now to this new life. It was his nature.

After a time, the old man forgot what he looked like. He saw himself only in the light of his Master's eyes, in the glances of the men he worked with, and of those who formed the human tide that flowed around him in the colony. He began to appreciate the invisibility of old age, the fading into the background, and the neutral distance of natural silence. He never told his story or confided in anyone. He gave his name only as Chacha, a common name for Uncle. Soon his quiet smile and gentle eyes became a canvas for listening, as he offered comfort from the anchor of his steady presence. He let the life of his fellow workers flow around him, and yet he was the first to notice a need or offer assistance. They learned to count on him just as others had in his old life. He discovered he hadn't changed that much after all. However his relationship with the world had become a living membrane of awareness of himself and his part in the life around him. His heart took on a pulse of aliveness that sheltered his soul longing.

As the winter passed, memories of his past life and his pilgrimage disappeared into the rhythm of living the teachings, of waking early to sit in meditation and to surrender to the gradual slowing into stillness, focus, and longing. The continuation of his meditation into his life and work flowed deeper than thought, more restful than feeling, and more true to his essential self.

He was more present, and yet he felt he was hardly there. It was as though his inner being was becoming light, transparent, and open. He marveled at how difficulties melted before this light, whether it was a cold wind, a heavy rain, a bruise, or the dull ache of fatigue at the end of the day. A shift to the inner light diminished sensation and caused a renewal that was not denial or repression but healing transformation. The cycle from spiritual practice to spiritual living became a circle of giving from an inner fountain that bestowed love continuously received, love continuously offered, and love continuously flowing.

And just as he discovered this cycle of renewal with fresh sight and new eyes, the old man saw himself as a part of a process. "I am the earth too," he thought, "I have been raised and shaped into a body, and now this body is slowly bending toward earth. And his acceptance of the cycles of life deepened, and he envisioned his life within a larger rhythm of mystic unfolding.

The red dust settled on him as he mixed the earth into mortar and poured it in molds to be baked in the ovens. He watched the trucks leave the brickyard piled high with bricks destined to become part of the walls, buildings, roads, walls, and drains of the Holy City. On their return, the trucks dumped broken old bricks into mounds that he and his companions broke into rubble. The red dust rose and settled on him as he hammered the bricks, staining his clothes, misting his beard, and dying him in the color of red earth.

The old man looked around at the brickyard, imagining what his son and daughter-in-law would think if they saw him wearing clothes stained by the red dust, his hands worn by labor, his face burned dark by the sun as he squatted in the brickyard. The memory of the morning he left his ancestral home rose to the surface of his mind and unraveled before his inner attention as if it were a story that belonged to someone else. Yet the story made him shiver, as if it contained the power of a myth and the mystery of deeper realities that energize the movements of change.

When he was a child, his parents managed his life and encouraged him to focus on his studies. They married him young, and his wife lovingly cared for him. He had always accepted this caring, preferring to please those he loved. He marveled at how he had moved within a finely tuned structure, playing his part as beloved son, devoted husband, provider, noble landowner, and government official. Abundance was natural. He never craved things because there was always more than enough. And yet, their caring spoiled him, separated him, and made him passive, used to compromise. He remembered how he yearned to play with the village children or sit with them by their fires under the night stars, but he never dared to ask and he was too afraid to go without permission.

The old man had always been supported by the structure of his family's wealth, tradition, and culture. Morning tea was served in his room, and meals were enjoyed with his family. If he wanted anything, there was always someone to bring it to him. His clothes were taken away by servants and returned, washed and ironed. His rooms were freshened in summer by colorful flower arrangements and moist curtains that cooled the air; and in winter, welcoming fires greeted him when he returned home.

The large house did not require his attention as family and servants managed its efficient rhythms. Money was provided for his marriage, private schools, university, and world travels, and yet his personal tastes were simple. He was dressed by his parents and then by his wife, without desiring his own style. He accepted furnishings bought by others and never cared which car his family chose for him. "And so it seems I am still doing the same thing here," the old man thought as he looked at the clothes that had been given to him.

He had enjoyed his family life because it was all he knew, but he had never experienced what he could be without them. He ignored his longings, pushing them aside until he forgot them, but the longings had waited within him. It seemed he had saved all his longings for the one great longing, the one he could not deny, the call of his soul.

The old man had experienced his wife's death as a slow drowning into grief. He had watched her fade as though the light of her being was being removed to another world. He had observed her rituals and devotions to her Hindu religion, but had remained untouched by her faith. She died as though she did not want to trouble him with her death, and her passing had felt like a slow dissolving of a link that had bonded them over fifty years, so he had not been prepared for the pain that followed her death. Unexpectedly, her death pulled him into a whirlpool of conflict that promised his own death. Yet out of that deeper drowning, a remembering of soul longing birthed the knowing that he must leave his home and make his death his own. Only then did the smile of grace shine on his release and open to the freedom of his seeking over the lands of northern India.

The remembering stirred up thoughts, feelings, attachments, and questions that felt like a haunting of ghosts, but the old man's steady work, regular spiritual practice, and the daily discourses of the Master strengthened his focus. Soon he felt more present than before, as if some anchor had settled him on this new ground, this new home.

Soon after, one spring day, when the freshly leaved trees were tossing in a brisk wind, the Master visited the brickyards, and as he walked around, he paused for a moment in front of the old man. As the old man met the Master's eyes, he entered a realm of benevolent compassionate radiance that eclipsed the world around him and opened his inner sight.

"So, you are still here?" the Master asked the old man with a gentle smile.

"Yes, Sire."

"From tomorrow you will report to the waterworks," the Master commanded, and the old man bowed, his hands folded at his heart.

Later that evening, a quiver of fear upset the old man's balance. Just as he had found his sense of belonging, he was commanded to move on. "Habit has served me well, but I cling to what I am used to and find it difficult to let go," he thought as he struggled within himself. "Just as the Master teaches, I am suffering from attachment and reaction, but the difference is that now I am aware of this and can strive to overcome these pulls."

The old man sighed, "It is nearly as hard to leave something I love as it was to leave a life that no longer gave me any pleasure. Then I had the passion of seeking to pull me forward. Now I do not want change. I do not want to serve in the waterworks. When will these tugs and pulls leave me? When will I be free to accept whatever changes come to me and surrender to them?"

THE WATERWORKS

As early spring moved toward summer, marking a full year since he had left his family home, the old man began his service in the waterworks of the Holy City. Resistance surged within him, and he longed for the dust and the bricks and the simple arts of pouring the molds or breaking down old bricks. He did not like the cold water, the sewage or the odorous drains, and he longed for the rhythm of the hammers.

Through the summer, he worked with the drains, pipes, and wells of the Holy City, but it took a season to release his missing of the brickyards, of what was no longer there and what he could no longer have. Because of the teachings of the Master, he was more conscious of the clinging that would not let go of the past, or allow him to accept his present circumstances. Just as he had struggled to release attachment to his loss of his parents and his wife and their way of life that was no more, he struggled with his nature and its likes and dislikes. As he deepened into feelings he had kept distant all his life, he discovered the child who had never complained, and the child who was afraid to make a fuss. He also discovered the promise of the child he had never been allowed to become.

The old man had never really thought about water. He washed his hands and face in the morning; soaked in a bath; stood under a shower; drank water or tea; but he had never cleaned anything. Water had always been his servant, but now he was the servant of water. He found the work repugnant and struggled with resistance. Although he entertained plans of escaping what was distasteful to him, he knew there was no purpose in leaving the Holy City. He shrank from the odors and sewage waste when the drains were plugged – breathing in gasps, turning his head away, and repeating his mantra – and strived to still his reactions by imagining how his family would welcome him if he returned home.

"If they had given me this work when I first came, I would have left," he muttered under his breath as he struggled with some odorous task.

The childish petulance that this work was beneath him fueled his longing to escape, and caused a surge of will to fight against these feelings with the only weapon he had, his spiritual practice. He persevered because he knew the loving light of the Master's eyes and his teachings were the truth, and this truth forced him to observe his reactions with clarity. As much as he detested the work, he knew he had to stay and see it through. His struggle with water returned him to memories of his departure from his ancestral home.

"All my life I avoided things I did not like," the old man admitted. "My position in life raised me above such work, but I also concealed distaste for the tasks of daily life. The work of others made my gracious, privileged life possible, but I took their work for granted. It grieves me now to think I did not give those who served me more appreciation."

Even as he struggled with his nature, he cherished the growth of awareness in his new life and sought to preserve the tender compassion that had blossomed during his travels. Slowly, he realized that his efforts to overcome his resistance had increased his discipline and given him a sense of being purified. Resistance made him aware of his arrogance, and so he searched within the chambers of his heart for release from the ties of attachment that led to judgment, and preferred choices. A part of him longed to be neutral, and to be able to accept whatever came before him.

As spring passed into burning summer, the old man's suggestions had improved the drains and reduced the blockages. He felt pride at how the network of pipes and drains that ran beneath the Holy City served the taps that welcomed pilgrims with fresh water as they washed the dust of the journey off their faces and hands and drank long and deep from the well. He watched *sevadars* pour water or *chai* into their cups in the *langar*, and delighted in their laughter when the pilgrims washed their plates and cups after eating. In the hostels, he heard the showers running and enjoyed seeing the new arrivals emerge refreshed and clean, ready to receive the bountiful blessings of the Master's teaching in the *satsangs*.

A sense of accomplishment lifted the old man's spirit because he realized that he contributed to those who lived there as well as to the welcome and comfort of the pilgrims. A new enthusiasm thrived in his service in the waterworks because he accepted that every task, however small or difficult, contributed to the abundant hospitality of the Master's Holy City.

With this attitude, water became entrancing to the old man. He observed the surges, ripples, and waves of water flowing through drains, bathrooms, kitchens, and laundries, and he listened to its gurgles, swishes, rushes, and rhythmic drippings and droppings as if it were music to his ears. He admired how the streets shone after early morning rains, and how the sun encouraged a gentle rising mist when the Master passed on his early morning rounds. The old man watched water flow into vast pots in the kitchen, where it steamed and bubbled and blended with lentils, spices, tea, vegetables, rice, oils, sugar, and flour, and sighed with satisfaction.

Water had many moods, and during cold spells he delighted in the frosting patterns on windows and the dusting gift of spare snow. He stood under the waterfall monsoons and celebrated the flooding of the streets. He also felt the love of water in the tears that fell from his eyes when he looked at the Master. The old man facilitated water's secret underground passage, and he rejoiced in its practical and joyous emergence into the life of the spiritual colony. He participated in the planning and the vigilant maintenance required to provide pure water to the Holy City's inhabitants and visitors, and he felt proud to be a servant of water.

As autumn fell once again toward winter, and the cold water and hard labor began to tell on the old man's body, he did not waver from his duties and love of water, though he moved more slowly, and he felt the aches and pains of the cold and damp more deeply. And then one morning, the Master looked at the old man and then spoke to one of his aides, and so it was that he received his instructions to report to the service of the fire in the *langar* kitchens.

THE LANGAR FIRES

TThe old man welcomed the chance to serve in the free kitchens of the *langar*. The magic of the fires that flamed beneath great copper vessels of *dal* and vegetables, burned under the hot metal plates that toasted the *chapatis* clapped into shape by the hands of radiant, singing women, and bubbled under the pots of boiling oil for the making of sweet *jalebis*, enchanted the old man. The *langar* fed all those who lived and visited the Holy City, and its production of food went on around the clock.

He took to fire with an immediate passion, as he had always longed to build fires, tend fires, and dream with fires. Unlike the changeable moods of water, fire was constant. While water adapted to influences, fire drew everything into it, transforming raw materials and releasing heat and energy. He loved the warmth, the colors, the sounds, and the vigilant attention required to protect fire from going out, or going out of bounds. He tamed fire. He formed it to his will, and his increasing focus was a reflection of his spiritual practice. Fire was pure joy for the old man because it made him feel like the child he always wanted to be – not the child of constraint but the wild child of freedom, the child that celebrated the beauty of nature and the elements, the child who inhabited his dreams.

And so it was that he entered the soaring song of the kitchens and the ever-rising flames that required consummate attention. The fires must be of an even heat, but not too hot. The fuel must be added at the right time after the appropriate selection of wood, rice husks, or dry grasses depending on whether it was *dal, chai,* vegetables or *chapatis*. The awakening of fire, its taming to perfection for the required task, its damping down and preserving of coals was mastered by subtle observation, constant adjustment, and fine attunement to both the fuel and the flame.

Fire became the old man's service of devotion. Inwardly and outwardly fire leapt upward, transforming fuel, resting but never going out, flaming under the ever-filling pots of *dal* and vegetables and the never-ending *chapatis* placed upon the hot griddles of the row of clay ovens. Once the *chapatis* were toasted, turned, and toasted again, they were lifted off the hot plates and thrown into baskets. Merry young girls carried the baskets on their heads, chatting and laughing, proud of their service, to a room where they emptied the *chapatis* onto a large white sheet. There, young men with glowing eyes brushed the *chapatis* with melted ghee so they would not stick together when they placed them by the thousands into spiral mounds to await the blessing of the Master.

As grains, produce and goods funneled toward the flame to be transformed into food and drink for residents and pilgrims, a steady stream of trucks arrived full of bags of grains, ghee, oils, vegetables, flour, sugar, and tea to replenish the supplies. The bags and boxes were carried to sheds and piled in stacks ready to be carried to the men and women *sevadars* who cut and chopped, and patted and stirred, preparing the foods for the fires. The cycle continued day and night in an endless stream of giving and receiving.

Laughing young men, sitting high on tractor seats above massive treaded tires, revved the rough, loud engines as they drove into the lanes between the ovens and fires to deposit wood and dry grasses from construction sites, and lands being cleared for orchards and gardens. At other times, the drivers deposited mounds of rice husks from a nearby mill that provided the dense, even heat for the vast copper cauldrons of golden *dal*.

Fire was essential to the alchemy of transformation for the grains, lentils, and vegetables that delighted the eyes and warmed the bellies of countless pilgrims. The free kitchen, the *langar*, was a miracle of love from a fountain of divine grace. All who participated in the river of loving nourishment were blessed by a love beyond all understanding, the love of participating in selfless giving and receiving.

The sounds of fire, the crackling as it gained strength, the roar of its power, and the smooth heart of the flame as it steadied, delighted the old man. Even though his focus was on the fire he tended, he also absorbed the loving, joyful activity around him. Women joked, chattered, sang and laughed as they cut vegetables, rolled the dough, and shaped the *chapatis* between their hands. Men of all ages and castes sang the songs of the saints as they stirred *dal, chai* and pots of boiling oil.

The roar of hearty flames – enlivened by the snapping of twigs and grasses that fed the fire, and by the rush of air that lifted sparks into the sky – was the living essence of the old man's service of love. His passion mingled with the fire that he tamed to perfection as he brought one cauldron of food to completion, only to begin another. When the Master blessed the food every morning after *satsang*, the songs of the *sevadars* soared like flames into the heart of heaven. The Master's glance of love set alight the souls of all who served in the kitchens of the Holy City into an even greater joy.

The old man tended his fire so that *chapatis* toasted to perfection, *dal* became the golden liquid of love, and *chai* the elixir of blessings. The songs of the women and the deeper men's voices rose like flames from faces radiant with joy, eyes shining, hearts radiating gratitude. The songs, the food, and the Master's blessings wove into a dream of love and the promise of a new world.

When the great *satsangs* were held and multitudes arrived, the old man lived by the fire day and the night, tending a clay oven fire for the *chapatis* through the hours of darkness, then stirring great cauldrons of *dal* and *chai* for breakfast. Through the day he built and tended dense, even fires to cook vegetables for the evening meal, before repeating the cycle. On Sundays, his fires boiled vats of oil for the making of sweet *jalebis*. The old man delighted in the smiles and laughter of the women as they dropped the dough into the oil and watched fantastic shapes emerge before removing them with their ladles. The heat carried a mist of sugar that crusted his beard, adding a dust of sweetness to his knowing that the *jalebis* would be placed before the Master for his blessing.

When the three o'clock siren sounded, the old man wrapped himself in his shawl and retreated into meditation. The inner and outer flames offered all that was needed for his sustenance. He often slept by the hearth, leaving the service of fire only for the call of nature and essential self-care. The Master came near daily when he blessed the food, and the *sevadars* knew that they must bring the old man meals or he would forget to eat in his passion for the fire.

When he repeated the mantra during his spiritual practice, he offered the words as fuel for transformation, and his love soared into his inner sky. This love merged into his outer world and became one with the songs, joy, and laughter of his spiritual companions. During the long days and nights tending the fires, he remembered images from his life as a householder: glimpses of women cooking over their village fires, farmers burning crops in their fields, and travelers circled around their fires as they sought warmth and protection. The fires of his life had been lit and tended by others who screened their heat and power. He had felt warmth from those fires, but they had never been as fierce or beautiful as the fires of the *langar*, and he had never been the fire keeper.

The heart of fire entered through the old man's skin into his bones, and his laughter knew no bounds. His longing surged like a roaring fire burning a path into his inner world. And then one day he understood that it had been the potential of fire hibernating in his long-abandoned roots of longing that had finally leapt free, giving him the clarity and will to leave his home and find his way to the Holy City.

The old man knew he was being prepared to leave his body and this world, but fear did not contract him. Like fire, he longed to merge into everything. He imagined his body falling like a husk into the fire, and his soul rising on the brilliant, flickering flames before vanishing into the mystery of the invisible spiritual realms.

GUARDIAN AT THE GATE

After a season in the service of fire, the old man was summoned to the Master's garden. He trembled when he heard the news because he felt another change was coming, and he did not want to lose the privilege of fire. When the Master's servant asked him to collect his belongings and bring them with him, his fear increased. "Would he be asked to leave? Would they want him to return to his family? Was he getting too old to offer service?"

The servant guided the old man to sit on a mat in the garden. Totally dependent on the will of his Master's love, the old man's innocent trust shone with a still humility that settled like an invisible sigh in the midst of the crowd surrounding the Master. After some time, the Master gestured to the old man to come closer and then offered him a bag of *jalebis*. The old man held the *prashad*, the blessed food, and waited. The Master looked at him with a gentle sweetness as he said, "Today you will move into the gatehouse, and offer your service with the guards at the entrance."

The old man bowed his head with his hands on his heart and said, "Thank you, Sire." Trembling, he opened the bag and put a *jalebi* in his mouth, marveling at the sweetness, with only one thought in his mind, "Now I won't have to go anywhere. Even my food will be eaten in this place. All I will ever need is here."

When the Master retired from the garden, and the guests began to disperse, one of the Master's *sevadars* showed him a small room by the gatehouse. The old man walked in and sat on the cot in wonder at the grace of this boon. And to think he had been afraid of losing the privilege of fire! One grace had simply replaced another. "Oh, would he ever learn to trust?"

The next morning when it was time to report for *seva*, an elderly *sevadar* led him to the guardhouse at the gate, gave the old man a stick and told him to look fierce. Though the idea of looking fierce made the old man laugh, he did as he was told and sat tall, and held the stick across his knees. A roof protected him from the sun, and he settled into an alert stillness that noticed everything but was part of nothing.

Ever vigilant, the old man guarded the gate to the Master's compound, bowing whenever the Master came and went. Like a stone in a river, he observed the stream of family, friends, servants, dignitaries, and supplicants arriving and departing. He checked their passes, sent requests to the Master's staff, and sometimes had to deny entrance. Soon, status, caste, gender, age, and position vanished in the stream of souls, and he understood that all were equal before the Lord. Those who passed him at the gate accepted the old man's fierce stillness and tall strength. They did not question his authority. He disappeared into the role of a guardian at the Master's gate, yet savored the relief of being personally invisible. Much of his time at the gate was free for meditation, so that his inner and outer worlds merged seamlessly. In one moment, he could be in deep inner attention and in the next, responding to a question.

"At last," he thought. "I have found my place." No memories of his past life rose to the surface of his mind, and he was content. As his new service focused on guarding the gate to his Master's home and office, he no longer needed to walk to the kitchens in service of fire, around the colony in service of water, or to the brickyard in service of earth. His life now rested like a stone, in surrender and acceptance on his seat in the guardhouse at the Master's gate. "Just as my body was weakening, the Master found a place for me. He knows what I need more than I do. He is taking care of me with the greatest love."

During this time of his inner and the outer life blending together, the old man's silence deepened. He became a point of stillness in a stream of coming and going. With his internal world anchored in meditation and his outer in loving devotion and service, the old man felt like he was turning inside out, that his envelope of skin and clothes was a covering for the hidden treasure of light fed by the fountain of his Master's love.

Although seasons passed, the old man

accepted them as the background for his glimpses of the Master's loving eyes. As he progressed more deeply into his inner life, that old man realized that discomfort was an unworthy distraction to his vigilance for soul light. This focus allowed him to adjust so that no time or energy was wasted on reaction or complaint.

The old man's countenance settled into neutral strength. When the Master passed, he bowed before him with tender respect, devotion, and love. And yet, if someone tried to enter the gate without permission – no matter how great the pleading, passion, or need – the old man's strength was immovable as a stone.

The old man witnessed the soul hunger of the pilgrims and supplicants, and saw that their longing for refuge was stronger than their pride, fear, or suffering. He respected the differences between young and old, rich and poor, male and female, and the privileges of position, wealth, caste, and family, yet the old man knew they were all souls seeking truth, love, and release from their burdens. And so he greeted each and every one with respect and kindness, guiding all to the Master, yet protecting the Master at the same time. He recognized that he was an extension of the Master's will and that every move he made, every thought, was in the service of His will.

With increased compassion, he remembered how he had begun to see the souls within each person, "I remember when I began to lose my edges," he thought as clouds of misting rain cocooned his guard hut. He pulled his shawl around him. "I remember when I wanted to become part of everything." Even though pictures of his pilgrimage wafted lightly in his mind, they faded before his internal focus like the fragrance of a dream, "but I never imagined then that I would become a part of Him."

THE MASTER'S GARDEN

After a cycle of seasons at the Master's gate, the old man sat before the Master for the yearly gifting of blessed food and clothing. Once again he trembled before a stirring of fear that he might be asked to leave, but the wave of love that surged as he bowed his head, hands folded in greeting, washed away all but the radiance of his Master's presence.

"You have been with us for some years now: first in the brickyard, then in the waterworks, followed by the *langar* kitchens, and now as a guardian at the gate?" the Master stated as a question.

The old man nodded, amazed that the Master remembered the details of his service in the colony. Overwhelmed by love, gratitude and awe, he lost all concern for outcome. When he heard the Master say it was time for him to move into the garden and become His personal servant, the old man bowed his head to His feet.

And so he moved from the gatehouse to a garden hut and became part of the Master's home and family – a quiet servant who supported the life that ebbed and flowed around the Master. Although he had regular duties, most often he anticipated what was needed. From earliest morning to late at night, the old man moved about the house and garden, being where he was needed, doing what needed to be done, and assisting all with quiet devotion.

One morning, he swept leaves after a night storm. The next, he was cleaning windows, potting flowers, clipping bushes, hosing pathways, or watering the garden. When guests arrived, he made tea and served trays of biscuits and water. Restoring confusion to order, and requests to satisfaction, he never complained or asked for anything. The Master's family spoke to him with affection, asking for their needs and wants respectfully.

"I am at peace," the old man thought. "I accepted my family life when I was loved by my parents and my wife, and did my best to be loving, kind and loyal, but when they died I could not live without love and care. I had to seek a spiritual path to find my way to the love of the Lord. Now I am content. I have fulfilled my purpose now that I have found the path to lead me to my soul."

When the Master was away, the old man prepared for his return. When the Master was in residence, he anticipated every need and attended to all his duties with full attention, yet he never intruded or interfered.

"I am seen only by the Master," he marveled, pleased that he disappeared from all interactions other than his service to his Lord, his family and guests. There was nothing he needed or wanted, so this invisibility was a gift that left him free to give his full attention to the great love within and without in the service of his Master.

In this way the old man passed several seasons – gently aging, slightly stooping, walking more slowly – yet the fierce light of his love and service combined with his innocent, pure trust made the old man appear younger, as though his soul were shining brightly, a reflection moon of the Master himself. He was the trusted servant who always knew what to do without being told. He rarely slept, preferring to sit in meditation whenever he was free. If he was needed, his devotion continued into his actions. Usually he opened his eyes seconds before a summons, as if he felt the call internally, so attuned he was to every movement and need of the Master.

"I belong to the Master so completely that I have become a part of Him," the old man said within himself, as he worked within the Master's compound.

Over time, the trusted servant's body weakened further, suggesting another change was coming near. The Master kept him close, asking him to bring fruit or warm milk, a blanket when the weather was cool, a fan when the sun was hot, or to remove his shoes so the Master could sit cross-legged in his garden chair.

"I am only in this body to serve my Master and put my best efforts into my spiritual practice. I have no other need or desire. Everything I need or want is here. I have everything I need."

No one discouraged the old man when he began to sit outside the Master's door. And no one said anything when he began to sleep there at night wrapped in his blanket and shawls. One day, he found an awning had been constructed to shelter him from the rain and sun, and a cot had been placed beside the wall.

The old man lived and breathed awareness of his Master's presence. All aspects of the old man's attention focused on the living connection between himself and his Master, inwardly and outwardly blending both presence and longing into exquisite joy. As the joy increased, his body seemed as though it would burst open and light would stream from his pores into the living air. And as the light intensified, it mirrored in the world around him. He saw through the cares and sufferings of the people, beyond their masks and roles, and their clinging to position and power, to the soul light longing to live through each person.

The old man's increased compassion also stirred a resistant fear that he knew only too well. "I find this fear of rejection at ever stage," he realized, and although the old man did not want to plunge once more into memories of his weaknesses, he knew he must find a way to release a lingering knot of separation that rippled from the echo of his past. As a fluttering of winged memories rose gently in his illuminated mind, he dove once more into his roots of fear. This time, the descent awakened realizations of how he had restricted his love. He felt shame at his memories of his family life as they rose to the surface of his mind in images and interactions that revealed clearly his fear of his father; his comfort from his mother's spoiling; his lack of appreciation of his wife's generous caring; his indifference to his son's enthusiasms; his disinterest in his servant's lives, and how he took them all for granted.

While he had never been angry or controlling, he had rarely been intimate. "I was formal because I was protecting myself. I cared more about myself than others. Oh, the shame of the holding back, and worse, I never realized the harm I did to others. No wonder my son went his own way," the old man mourned.

"I escaped into my work because it gave me a sense of worth, and because it pleased my father, but I lost the capacity for passion. If it had not been for my wife, my life would have been dry and empty. When we long for love, why do we hold back? When we need love, why do we fear it? When we have love, why do we fear losing it? I must find a way to release the fear and open to the love. I must not hold back any longer from offering all that I am. I must learn how to open to receive all that is being given."

Memories surfaced of himself as a young child. "I lived to please my father, and I was always afraid I would lose his love if I did anything wrong," he realized. "My father was noble and powerful, and he expected me to be like him. He never let me be a child. He thought he was doing his best, but he never let me find out who I was. I lost myself in pleasing him. And now I am doing my best to please the Master, and I fear I am repeating the same pattern. Yet I feel this spiritual Father is allowing me to release this fear through my spiritual practice and the realizations that come to me. Oh how I long to release this tangle of fear and open to the love."

The old man faced the residue of his human failure and its influence on his ability to merge with the love of his soul. Frustration rose like a flame, and he wept with a sorrow so passionate that it stunned him. How he longed to wipe away these tendencies to hold back, to limit love, and to refuse to open.

The old man's personal life had vanished during his seasons of service in the Holy City, so it was alarming for him to suffer the return of his past life. Even so, he surrendered in humility and bore the burden of the shame that surfaced in his heart and mind, because he understood that the roots of his nature were being opened before his soul-light to flower before his consciousness, and find their way to release.

"All that was formed by my conception, birthing, and living is preparing for release," he whispered to the sighing branches of the trees in the Master's garden. As this truth translated into his body, a wave of compassion for his weaknesses made him tremble, and he leaned against the garden wall of the Master's compound.

"When was there ever time to know these things in my family life?" he cried within himself, seeking forgiveness, feeling awe before the inner light that seemed to see all, yet accept all. "When the time came, I felt the call of my soul and left all that had been my life so that I could find my way here." With these realizations, his heart expanded toward the divine love that was preparing him to receive an even greater love.

Summer approached with fearsome heat. The old man's breathing labored, and he felt dizzy at times, but he never complained. He moved more slowly but never failed in his duties, although he trembled when he served the Master tea and knelt more slowly when he bent to slip off the Master's sandals. Although he never complained and did his best to endure his increasing discomfort, silently, passionately, he begged within himself, "Oh, Lord, this body is wearing out. When will I be released?"

The burning heat of the sun intensified, and the earth pulled at his body. The garden became a mirage. Figures moved as if in a dream. Voices faded into the background. As the old man's devotion merged with the inner light, the soul of the old man burned brightly, and he began to slip from the world. The light from within shone brighter than the burning of the sun, and the old man felt his life had been one endless stream of longing toward this time of soul radiance. He imagined the soul rays of his family and of all beings streaming toward their release from the world, and glimpsed a greater plan. The weaving of the soul rays of his parents, wife, and son with his own, and all those that he had known in this lifetime, blended together in a pattern of shared human joys and sorrows.

The revelations at the roots of his being continued as memories of his family relationships revealed the karmic threads of giving and receiving and the cause and effect of actions and reactions. He allowed all to be exposed with weary humility, recognizing the helplessness he had always known and realizing that although this helplessness had been his weakness, it was now his strength. The willingness to be vulnerable was also a release at the gate of his soul. Whatever thoughts he had about himself, whatever memories of shame or loss, the old man knew all must release as an offering of his fluttering, winged self, as if his complex of mind, heart, and body were woven of feathers that had sustained his cocoon of ignorance and must now fly free.

And then, as he realized that his surrender to death was an active offering, not just a passive receiving, he participated more fully in the rooting of his nature; in exposing his hidden fears; in opening his secrets locked within himself, and in ending any illusion that he was not this or that.

Gratitude surged when he understood how his family had protected him from the potential of his dark self. His father's loving discipline and his mother's emphasis on tradition, duty, and regularity had prepared him to accept the nurturing management of his wife. Together, his family had been the walls of the river of his life, keeping him contained, keeping him safe. His parents believed in the nobility of their way of life, and although they had held him prisoner, he saw that he also had held them prisoner in the same way. They had moved through life together, serving each other, playing their roles. Together they filled their days with the efforts and fruits of dignity, kindness, and tolerance. There was no one to blame and everything to be thankful for. The old man's good life had led to his freedom, and his love for his family had led to an even greater love.

"How many more tears must I shed before I drop this bag of bones?" he asked the night sky, but there was no answer. "This business of being human is a strange business indeed. There were no classes in my schools for facing the mystery of death and my soul, but now I have the example of the Master to inspire and guide me. It is my journey, my pilgrimage, my adventure, my exploration, and my experience that opens the path to my soul, but it is also the Lord's, as he has been within me all this time. The Master's love inspires me, but it is up to me to have the courage to open to the love, and the light that is stronger and brighter than anyone can imagine. How long before I can see and know my own divine self that has always been a part of me?"

"I am old in this body, but I am young before this soul light," the old man said. Aware of how others must see him as an elderly, stooping servant, he chuckled, "But no one knows what's going on inside me. Even a short time ago, I never could have imagined that I would experience this internal aliveness, or enter into a spiritual journey within myself." Once more, he offered gratitude for the shelter the Master had granted him in the Holy City.

"The pilgrimage never stopped when I received refuge from the Master and was welcomed to live and serve in the Holy City. My journey and my seeking continued with the spiritual practice," he realized. "This is an even greater adventure, more than I ever imagined, but I am ready to let go."

As ready as the old man was to merge with his soul and gain release from his body, each morning when he awoke he accepted that he had one more day to prepare for his passing. His service to the Master alternated with an internal light of consciousness that exposed his nature and its clinging to the world. All that was dark and hidden within him was brought into the light. The old man knew that it was through the remnants of fear, desire, will, and longing that the path would open, so he fought the darkness within himself with his spiritual practice to lead it to the light.

"I can no longer be asleep to myself," he determined. "I must know all of my self." And then he would be summoned to the Master for some small task and he would look into His eyes and know that the path of love was opening beyond all that held him back. "Am I doing anything?" he questioned within. "When I look in His eyes I feel it is all a gift, a grace from Him. Even now, I know nothing. I understand nothing, and that is the way it is. All love, all trust, all surrender. That is all there is."

Wherever he focused his attention, effort waited. Sometimes awe would be so great, he would fall senseless before the light, asking forgiveness and begging to forgive all, so that he could be free of the weight of his ignorant darkness. The burning heat of the high summer sun intensified until the longing for rain and coolness became one with his longing for union with his soul. He felt the imminent death of his aged body, but his longing felt like a cry of hunger of a newborn child. His body suffered increasing weakness, dizziness, and his consciousness distanced from the life around him. Yet the combined memories and realizations continued to ignite in his mind as if there were no end to fire.

"I lived on the surface of life, gliding through, never feeling too deeply, never suffering too much, even when my parents passed," the old man remembered. "I honored the completion of their life journey with proper respect and ceremony, but I did not mourn them with my heart. My wife took care of all the arrangements. I was like a bystander, someone who showed up when everything was done. They made everything easy for me. Was I a person who needed to be protected? Or was it a habit she continued because I was the cherished son and only child? I hid from grief like I hid from love until my wife passed. Then I broke open and dropped into a current of grief that was so powerful I was helpless before it. The pain was stronger than my role, my mask, and my armor against my true self."

And then there was a time when he felt that

all that he knew was being evacuated from his being, as though illuminated space was the only quality that must remain. "Such a separating of heavy and light, such a relief of burdens releasing, such a lifting of guilt from my heart," the old man observed. "It is like the separation of cream from milk. I am being evacuated from myself and I can only give thanks that it is not as uncomfortable as it could be."

Even within this dying, the old man gave thanks that he was able to perform his duties. He focused his attention within and felt uplifted by the illumination of increasing love. "I am like the horse who wants to run the last few yards to the stable. I feel I am ready to go and yet I must make best use of every day that He gifts to me. I must trust that He knows the right time for my passing."

In the Master's garden, in the burning heat of summer's cauldron, when all existence begged for moisture and coolness, the old man's memories uncovered the luminous seed of yearning adoration he had felt as a child whenever a holy man visited or a *sadhu* sought alms in his ancestral home. He remembered the pull he had felt to sit at their feet, but had always subdued the urge with an embarrassment born of fear. From the early beginnings of his life, the old man realized he had believed he could not have what he really wanted, whether it was sitting around the fires with the village children, or following the impulse to be closer to the holy men. The old man was grateful that even forgotten longings have their time of harvest.

His body became a weight, as though gravity had already claimed him. He fought this weakness to rise in the morning, to get up off a chair, and to walk short distances without gasping for breath. Although his body felt heavier, he had lost weight. He seemed almost transparent in his lightness. "It must be my bones that are heavy," he thought. "Perhaps they long to lie at rest or melt in the funeral pyre, just as I long to fly free."

The old man's realizations continued with internal dialogues that attempted to forgive, understand and release his past. "Now I see that my natural inclinations and impulses were suppressed, my joy curtailed, and my longings delayed until they disappeared. With their loss, I also lost my authentic feelings. I was trained for duty and to follow tradition, and there was great value and love in our family life. However, along with the privileges there were sacrifices. When soul longing carried me away from my ancestral home, I opened a new chapter of my life. For the first time I was free to become my true self."

His thoughts flew to his son. "I must write him a letter and tell him about all that has happened to me. Why have I not done this before?" he groaned. Then, with trembling hands, he penned a letter, folded it and wrote the address of his ancestral home on the paper. Emotions overwhelmed him as an even deeper realization that he would never see his family or his home gathered in his heart and body.

"I am like a leaf being shaken free of a tree. Oh, son, please forgive your father," he cried from his most innermost heart.

Remnants of the roots of his earthly ties offered themselves to release. He saw that his father, mother, wife, son, and everyone he had ever known had been one of the many faces of love, one of the faces of the divine. There was no longer any need for shame because he understood the different stages of his life had to unfold just as they had, with limited consciousness in each stage, with an unknowing of the next stage to come. At each step, he had moved on. He longed to let go and receive the soul love that was opening in ever-brighter illumination. As the tumult of feelings subsided, peace entered his heart.

As the inner light increased, the old man became aware of an entrance, as if space were opening into a grand dominion. His point of consciousness recognized that he had arrived at the gate to the true Holy City, the home of his soul. But he could not pass the guardians at the gate. There was still more work to do before he would be free.

For a time an internal soul-brightening continued within the old man: illuminations rising and letting go, tender forgiveness and forgiving, relief of forgetting, and sweet freedom from shame and guilt rising toward a crescendo of stillness. As the light increased, meditation continued with the focus on the inner Lord of the Soul. Conscious dying blended effort with ever-increasing grace toward communion with his divine source. Like a bird, the two wings of effort and grace worked together to create the beauty and power of the old man's internal flight.

At times, exhaustion held him prisoner in frozen time, and the tide of his mind spread into emptiness while his body felt as heavy as concrete. At other times, grace transported him to a luminous ocean, and his body became as light as a feather. These variations were all temporary, changing from one to another, until his only longing was for what would not change, for the time when grace and effort merged until there was no separation, no Master and no disciple. Just as days and nights of relentless, burning heat offered no respite to his aged body, his inner practice offered no rest from his process of release.

Exploring thoughts, emotions, and memories required intense focus because the old man knew any reaction would pull him into dangerous, deeper currents of fear, attachment, or will that would hold him prisoner in his body and his mind. As he dug into his roots, his soul soared as if the patterning of nature participated in his tree of life. He felt himself growing both downward and upward at the same time, toward some sense of offering, as though death could be a spontaneous combustion, a burst of a seedpod, or a dropping of ripe fruit.

The world continued to fade as the inner light grew stronger, and the old man opened with tears, trembling, and gratitude. Every moment was intense effort, intense longing, and intense grace, as if his inner state were a gift of consciousness that carried an insatiable longing for more. His body weakened.

He often felt dizzy, as the heat of the outer world met the heat of the inner world. He felt as though he was in the hands of forces he could not fully comprehend.

"It must be what the mystics describe with their examples from daily life. We are beaten like the cloth the washer man pounds by the river until we are cleansed. We are shaped from within and without like the clay pot on the potters wheel until we are prepared to receive. We are hammered in the fire by the ironmonger until we are strong. Somehow I never realized this before. It has always been the hand of the divine working with me, supporting me, helping me let go. Oh, the love that is in this world and how long it took me to see it and know it! To give love and receive love! To not be afraid of love!' the old man exclaimed in awe.

"But perhaps that is the way it is," he comforted himself. "An embryo in the womb of his mother cannot imagine the person he is destined to be, and perhaps it is the same with the embryo soul. We sense and participate in this unfolding toward something we long for and also fear, and yet we cannot really know what that is until we are there. And yet there is a trust and love that carries us through."

And then, when the world around him seemed as though it would ignite in flames from the burning heat, blessings fell like rain. The monsoon arrived on a burst of wind from the Himalayas and shocked the trees into a moaning flailing against a fearful, orange sky. Whirling dust fled before the advancing storm. The temperature dropped, thunder rumbled, and lightning shot the night bright with heavens' branching. The earth received the offering as the old man stood his ground under the weight of falling water, giving thanks for renewal, for dying, and for love.

Later that night, the old man sat at his Master's door, his shawl wrapped around him, his eyes closed, no longer aware of the tumultuous monsoon. The inner pull was so strong that an upward current caught him and carried him into singing radiance. With joy he surrendered, and his soul soared free of his body with a sigh as it opened into the inner song, a fragrant offering to love.

After the old man's passing, sevadars found this letter and mailed it to his son:

My dear son,

I send my dearest love to you and your family.

As I approach my passing from this body and this world, I find I wish to tell you about the journey that brought me to this Holy City where I am spending my last days.

Please forgive me for any distress caused by my sudden departure from our ancestral home. I was unable to tell you of the strong need that had arisen within me to seek and find a spiritual path and a teacher to guide me toward my passing, as I was afraid you would beg me to stay. I knew I would not be strong enough to explain or defend my wish to leave, and so I left without informing you.

For several months, until the winter cold, I wandered as a *sadhu* over our northern lands, and I tell you sincerely, that these months of living simply, sleeping on the ground, enjoying fires under the stars, and meeting the peoples of our country from many walks of life were the most happy of times. Such adventures, your old father enjoyed. I was taken care of so many times, by kindness, generosity, and friendship. I learned so much about myself, about life, about death, and most of all about trust.

Just as I had given up, I was led to a Holy City where I have been living these past two plus years. I arrived at this refuge of truth and was given shelter by the great soul who illuminates this City with His grace and Holy presence. I have given service and practiced the meditation and find myself at peace as I prepare for my passing.

All my life, out of a sense of duty, I put aside my spiritual yearnings. I did not find satisfaction in our family rituals, but my heart always stirred whenever the *sadhus* and holy men came to our door. After your dear mother's passing, I followed my heart and my journey led me to this holy place.

My dear, dear son, if you have such a yearning, please follow this yearning while you are raising your family, and working in this busy world. If you can come to this place and learn where your father passed his last days, and see for yourself the true home of his soul, I would be very pleased.

It gives me great happiness to let you know of the peace and joy I feel as my time nears. I am so very thankful to my father and mother, and all those before who provided such a good life for me. My eyes fill with tears at the thought of my beloved wife and all she gave to me, and of our years raising you in a home full of love. We were fortunate in every way. And yet, even with all this good fortune, I had a need to find and follow the path to my soul, in a way that felt true and right.

As I await this most longed for union with my soul, I close now with heartfelt love, your Father.

GLOSSARY

Bhajan – devotional song of a mantra, poem or complex poetic musical offering

Chai – Masala chai is a tea blended with a mixture of aromatic Indian spices and herbs

Chai Walla – a worker in India who makes or delivers Masala chai tea

Chapati – Indian flatbread that accompanies food

Dal – preparation of dried beans, lentils that have been stripped of outer hulls and split and cooked with spices to accompany rice, vegetables and other Indian dishes.

Dharma – one's righteous duty on a virtuous path; that which upholds and supports as law in caste, religion and social position.

Ganja – slang terms for marijuana

Hanuman – the mighty monkey God in the Hindu pantheon

Haveli – enclosed private mansions around a courtyard with a fountain garden, and a gate

Jalebi – Indian fried sweet made by deep-frying batter in various shapes then soaking them in syrup.

Ji – a respectful term to add after a name.

Kurta – loose shirt worn by both men and women over a variety of loose-fitting pants

Langar – a community vegetarian free kitchen where all eat as equals in the open air.

Lungi – South Indian wrap-around woven cotton cloth worn as a skirt by both men and women in Kerala; also known as a *dhoti* in Hindi, in Northern India.

Namasté – greeting salutation meaning "I bow to you" or "I honor the Light within you," accompanied by a slight bow made with hands pressed together, palms touching and fingers pointed upwards, in front of the chest – the *Añjali Mudrā* – offering respect.

Neem tree – known as "The Divine Tree" as it offers many medicinal properties

Pathi – places where God resides or the person who sings sacred *shabds* during *satsangs*

Prashad – food blessed by a spiritual teacher and given to devotees

Puja – a ceremony of gratitude or a religious ritual performed as an offering to various deities, distinguished persons, or special guests.

Radha Soami – Lord of the Soul

Rajasthan – largest state of the Republic of India encompassing most of the area of the large, inhospitable Great Indian Desert (Thar Desert) in north west India; capital Jaipur.

Sadhu – common term for mystics, ascetics, yogis, and wandering monks who are dedicated to achieving their spiritual liberation.

Satsang – gathering of seekers of truth to share discourses and chanting to inspire divine love consciousness of a devotee in the company of a guru or enlightened teacher

Seva – service; compassion in action.

Sevadar – offers service without thought of reward

Shabd – words or devotional poems or songs

Tiffin – metal lunch containers for carrying hot food in India

Tuk Tuks – open auto rickshaws

Walla – a worker who performs a specific task

AUTHOR

The story of the old man arrived as a dream that was rich and deep in extraordinary clarity during a visit to my spiritual colony in India twelve years ago, in 1999. The dream left me trembling in bliss at the sincerity of a humble soul seeking his release under the guidance of a spiritual teacher with a spiritual practice of meditation, moral living, and service. Several times I told the story to dear friends, but it would not leave me, and so I began to write it down. The writing of the dream has been joyful, uplifting and inspiring, as well as challenging. Expressing what is rarely shared – the interior journey of a struggling soul – has been a process of service, dedication, and of awe. I offer it as inspiration to those who long to be released from fear, and to open to their passing from this world as a spiritual adventure, a pilgrimage of longing, and a journey of the soul.

The focus of every journey to India has always been to sit at the feet of my spiritual teacher, devote time to meditation, attend *satsang*, and enjoy the company of spiritual companions. I arrive early to recover from the journey, and I stay longer to savor what I have received in my spiritual retreat before returning to my busy life. I believe in gradual transitions, and it is this approach to travel that has given the time and space to explore India. During my travels, I meet people from all walks of life, and I cherish the memories of all the many and varied experiences that helped me to know the peoples and lands of India.

Today, as I write about The Old Man & His Soul, it is exactly thirty years since my first trip to India in October 1979. My excitement was mixed with fear, as I was a young mother at the time, and I was traveling alone. The view from the plane of Delhi in the early morning seemed harsh in the grey misty dawn, but when I stepped off the plane, my first welcome was the scent of India. This first breath was uniquely satisfying to my heart and soul, and as my feet touched the ground, I felt as though I was coming home to Mother India.

After customs, I was met by a *sevadar* from my spiritual path holding a sign with my name on it upside down. As we drove through the misty early dawn, the road was packed with vehicles of all descriptions. My eyes opened wide as we passed shawl-wrapped figures bicycling alongside thundering rows of exotically painted trucks, the occasional lumbering elephant decorated with mirror trappings, boys selling flower garlands, wandering cows, and *chai wallas* sleepily lighting up their stoves, all blending together in the misty, early morning New Delhi sunrise.

At the *Radha Soami Satsangar*, the management offered me a breakfast of cornflakes, toast and *chai*, then assigned me a room where I could refresh myself and rest for a few hours. After lunch, I shyly approached women sifting through rice and sorting *prashad* into small bags. They invited me to help them, and although we did not speak the same language, their bright eyes, sweet smiles and laughter welcomed me into their circle.

In the evening, the *sevadars* led me through the chaos of the train station to my stateroom and soon I was heading north toward north toward my spiritual colony near the foothills of the Himalayas in Beas, near Amritsar. My excitement and fatigue, combined with the rhythm of the train, the stops along the way in the dark of night where I saw travelers hunched around fires or sleeping on the ground, produced a euphoria that would not let me sleep. And so, in the early dawn, I stood in the passage by the window, waiting for the first glimpse of the spiritual colony where I would stay for the next six weeks. As we crossed the Beas River, I glimpsed the domes of the *satsangar* reflecting the colors of a glorious crimson sunrise. I had arrived at the destination I had dreamed of ever since I was a child – a Holy City.

In my spiritual colony, our teacher advises us to, "Die while Living." Our daily spiritual practice helps us live a path that takes us beyond the fear of death to the life of the soul. The spiritual teacher lights the path with the example of His blessed presence, and gives us the teachings and the practice to rise out of suffering, reaction and desire into surrender and contentment, and above all, to support our conscious preparation for our death with devotion to a spiritual practice.

It was during one of these visits about twelve years ago that the dream of 'The Old Man & His Soul' was gifted to me. To me, it was a dream of profound immersion in color, detail and presence. It was a dream that became part of me, and a dream that taught me many things. I share this dream of an old man, knowing that it is also the dream of our soul, to return to our true home.

I would also like to say that this dream takes place in an imaginary India, the India of our dreams, the Indian landscape of our hearts. So I ask forgiveness of the reader if this India does not match the customs or realities of one of the northern states of India, because in truth, this story encompasses them all.

My teacher always says, "The Lord longs for you more than you long for him." If that is true then it must be a great longing indeed. So let us all, as embryo souls, long with all our heart and soul to open to our spiritual life, the great life of our soul, and prepare to receive this great longing and this great love from the Lord of our Soul.

OTHER BOOKS BY FARIDA SHARAN

Herbs of Grace – Becoming Independently Healthy

Creative Menopause –
Illuminating Women's Health and Spirituality

Iridology – A Complete Guide

Flower Child in the Summer of Love
A sixties spiritual seeker's psychedelic saga

Iridology Coloring Book (co-author Ghatfan Safi)

Dictionary of Iridology (co-author Ghatfan Safi)

All books available from:

School of Natural Medicine International
Boulder, Colorado USA

www.purehealth.com
www.faridasharan.com
www.independentlyhealthy.typepad.com

faridasharan@purehealth.com
faridasharan@gmail.com

Made in the USA
Charleston, SC
28 July 2010